D0660567

CARLOS VELÁZQUEZ

THE COWBOY BIBLE
AND OTHER STORIES

Translated from
the Spanish by Achy Obejas

RESTLESS BOOKS
BROOKLYN, NEW YORK

First published in Spanish as *La Biblia Vaquera* by
Editorial Sexto Piso, Mexico City, 2011
Digital edition published by Restless Books, 2016
This edition published by Restless Books, 2016

Cover design by Rodrigo Corral
Set in Garibaldi by Tetragon, London

Library of Congress Cataloging-in-Publication
Data: Available upon request.

ISBN: 978-1-63206-022-8

Printed in the United States of America

Ellison, Stavans, and Hochstein LP
232 3rd Street, Suite A111
Brooklyn, NY 11215
www.restlessbooks.com
publisher@restlessbooks.com

CONTENTS

For Celeste Velázquez,
red-beaked little white dove

I could see the big neon Bible all lighted up on the preacher's church. Maybe it's lighted up tonight, too, with its yellow pages and red letters and big blue cross in the center. Maybe they light it up even if the preacher isn't there.

JOHN KENNEDY TOOLE
THE NEON BIBLE

San Pedrisco
San Pedro Sky
Monterreycillo
Saltillo
Goméz Pancracio
San Pedroosvelt
Moncloyork
San Pedroslavia
Cuatrociénegas
San Pedrostuttgart
San Pedro Amaro de la
Purificación, Bahía
San Pedrosburgo
Monterrey
San Pedro Garza García
Estación Marte
San Pedrinho
Los Ramones, Nueva León

PopSTock!

FICTION

THE COWBOY BIBLE

For José Alfredo Jiménez Ortiz

I WAS BORN IN A CORNER. In a wrestling ring. At Gómez Palace. I'm Lagunero. I'm *rudo*—a thug, a rascal. I'm a Menace.

I've always lived in San Pedro Amaro de la Purificación, in the state of Coahuila. The best Western of my childhood—*Rue des Petites Epicuros*, Paris, July of 19**—starred my father, masked, playing his old plastic sax on top of the ring. His name was Eusebio Laiseca, but he was known that night in Belgrano as Menace I, an RCA corporate shareholder. In addition to being a Greco-Roman wrestler and having a weakness for Raquel Welch's ass, he formed part of the famous *norteño* duo, El Palomo and El Gorrión.

I first stepped in the Laguna Olympic Arena when I was five years old. I still remember my father, his back flat against the canvas, improvising some free jazz with his double quartet. That day, between the twelve strings and the four corners, before Don Cherry could jump off a post with his toy trumpet, I bared my obsessions. The first, the barrier created by my father's mask (the mask he wore to fight was like a *burladero*, a wall that shelters fleeing bullfighters), and the second, the Bible he gave me when he defeated Santo, the Silver Mask. A Latin American paperback, bound in denim. A beauty, its color ranging from the intensity of Blue Demon's mask to a Levi's 501 fade. My father baptized it The Cowboy Bible* and I couldn't let it go. It became my security blanket. I was the new Linus. The Linus of the neon ring.

At sixteen, I saw two junkies die: Menace I and Menace II. My father left me his masks, his cape and his boots, handmade courtesy of some Anglosexual groupies. I didn't drop out of school. I had a degree in analysis and in the discrepancies between Side B, the bonus track, and the hidden track. One night, as I was working on my thesis about the influence of MP3 technology on imitation

* a.k.a. The Country Bible.

wrestler suits, El Joven Murrieta announced the return of a legend on the ten o'clock news, the headlining appearance of Santo's Son. That's when I climbed into the ring.

I debuted Sunday, December 21st. My godfather was Yelero Aguilar. A semifinal match. Australian relievers. The Ministers of Death I and II and Menace Jr. versus Tony Rodríguez, The Gentleman Falcon, and Little Falcon. Referee: Sergio Cordero.

We climbed into the ring accompanied by international cheerleaders. The Cousins, a female group from Argentina, sang, *Watch your hands, Antonio, 'cuz Mama's in the kitchen.* Depeche Mode's Never Let Me Down Again played in the background. That's when I discovered my wrestling style, what would later be called Neo Vulgar Retro Kitsch. The kind of experimentation that had me playing Ministry with Rocío Banquells and Los Ángeles Negros, Los Terrícolas, and Los Caminantes, with María Daniela y Su Sonido Lasser.

No wrestling arena ever has AC, parking, or clean bathrooms. Since I had won the First contest at the Coahuila 2002 facilities with a set of cages I called First Adolescents, the critics called me a fan of Technologic, Daft Punk's new video. Another group that was not too upset about my scandalous rise in popularity called me the boy genius of Lagunero painting.

The Cowboy Bible is like Black Mathematics or like a Little Brown Book. Before each match, I'd open the Bible in the dressing room in front of an altar dedicated to Yemayá, Eleguá, Changó, Ochún, and Obatalá. As a sacrifice I would offer up whatever pop single was playing on the radio and then I'd eat a chicken heart. When it came to Santería, I was privileged. The Cuban gods protected me in combat.

Because Gómez Palacio has always been the exquisite and proud birthplace of so many celebrity wrestlers, my solo and group shows grew in proportion to my detractors. The boxing and wrestling commissioner, in a sublime move, sentenced me to tour the Torreón-Gómez-Lerdo circuit.

The Ministers and I were victors everywhere. At the Municipal Auditorium, the crash cathedral, we unmasked the masked Diaboliques I, II, and III. They were triplets who worked at a butcher shop in downtown Gómez Patricio. My agent, making sure we had a dramatic lineup, got us a stellar fight, our last as the Three Musketeers, because he knew I needed to abandon the classic power trio format—bass, drums, guitar—in order to launch myself as a soloist.

My first individual performance was at the Laguna Coliseum. Wrestling fans are no different than film fans or ballet buffs. They are dying to say fuck you to the referee, to piss on the linesman. That's when I started to suffer from withdrawal. It happened during hand-to-hand combat against the Great Markus. In the darkness of my dressing room, naked and possessed, I had sacrificed a Mecano single. I was going through cold turkey because of The Ministers' absence. As I climbed into the ring, I showed the Cowboy Bible off to the audience, to the firefighters, to the cops, to the press. I put my hand on my heart and promised to abide by Murphy's Law. The bell rang and the Great Markus said, Just take off your shitty little Wranglers and let's play billiards. I won by knocking him down, twice. The first and second time.

My opponents were always rudos or exotics. My manager and Little Saint Jude Thaddeus—all that yakking's gonna win you a smacking—said that a gladiator like me, who can take on Whoppers and Dagwoods with ease, should not waste his talents on conventional choreography. Blood should splatter the seats and stain the blonds.

The existential angst trailing these little rubber wrestlers who'd never even broken out of their packaging moved me to write and positioned me not only as the city's youngest visual art critic but, to date, the only one. My column, Contemporanea, is still running Thursdays in the *Milenio Laguna* newspaper. As arbiter of visual arts, I was unsparing. I became a local tyrant.

My next exhibition was at the Plaza de Toros. I confronted Blue Panther, the Lagunero teacher. An italic rain was falling at the start of the show, and the lusty ring girls refused to go out without an umbrella. I left the dressing room holding an inflatable doll. The ovation was thunderous. It looked like Santos Modelo territory, headquarters for the Santos Laguna Warriors. There hadn't been anything like this in wrestling since Hurricane Ramírez went out with Tonina Jackson. The Plaza is an appropriate place for experimentation. The bullring arena and the elements allow for a greater expansion of jazz-rock fusion and for trying out a few things with funk.

A mini-tour through San Pedroslavia and Pancho I. Mamadero prepared me for a more extensive trek through the barrio sands of Piernas Negras, San Pedrosburgo, Monterrey, and Estación Marte. I played almost every position: catcher, center fielder, and soliton. I was ready to take part in a riot of atomic magnitude to benefit the Red Cross, and I owed everything to my manager and the Holy Child Anacleto.

Because of my nasty glamor skills at the mixer, the turntable and scratching, the Public Records Office proposed giving me the state youth award. I was up against artists, rockers, writers, but the sitting government gave it to me for my timeless contributions to the people's welfare. Still, a vocal community protested—especially the tiny frivolous faction of distinguished society ladies I called The Casserole Vanguard and reviled as chewy Ponderosa-brand wieners, uptight damsels who raised the profile of the engraving workshop to the rank of artistic affiliation. Then they just gave the award to a wrestler. A rudo. It was so fucked up, they should have given it to Martín Mantra.

Naturally, the award gave me the air of a pop star. The kind of envy provoked by all Laguneros inspired my detractors into even more taunting, and they gave me an appropriate, unbeatable, leonine nickname that was the truest of all: La Diva.

The battle between the volunteers for the Oblivion Cross was scheduled for Gomitos. At the Olímpico

Laguna. A deluxe finale. Vintage relievers. Santo's Son, Fishman, Doctor Wagner, and Aquarius versus Scarlett Pimpernel, Sexypisces, Super Super Super Super Porky, Silver Arm, and Menace Jr.

In order to tend to the son of the guy who filmed the psalms as if he were a favorite Taco Bell client, I drew a pentacle on my dressing room door and dropped a Mariana Ochoa CD in the middle. When I found out I'd be playing a few arm-wrestling tournaments with my foremost rival, I appealed to all the magic a *santero* wrestler can scramble up on Skype.

As was to be expected by now, I appeared onstage with the Cowboy Bible held high. For ambient sound, there was Juan Salazar's rendition of Amor de la calle. The fight was filmed for television. Wrestling's heavy division meets wrestling's heavy division. The fight got ratings that rivaled religious fanatical DJs. We were disqualified. To the beat of rudos rudos rudos, Dr. Assassin leapt from the second row dressed in civilian clothes, and we kicked Santo's Son's ass until we tore his mask and confiscated the martyr's blood, urged on by the screams of the crowd: Fuck him, fuck that fucking dwarf.

I took the mic for our team and challenged Santo's

Son. Every saint deserves a chapel. The crowd. The crowd. I dared him to risk his belt. The defeated dwarf came up to the booth and grabbed the mic. I accept. I accept, Menace Jr. You're nothing. You're only good with a team. Menace Jr., by yourself, you are nothing. With those love handles of yours, no surgeon will take you on. You're nothing.

The silver dwarf's many performance dates had the promoters scheduling our show for after he got back from a two-month tour of Japan with Savoy Brown. My agent and little Saint Jude Singsong concluded we had to do some maintenance on our equipment, get a new life preserver, oil the joints, and change some of the padding. The point was to make a profit. And to get in shape after the insult about my weight and show up at the gig with more experience under my belt.

The first prized mask I grabbed was the Purchase Award at the DCCCXLVIII New Art Biennale in the state of Coahuila. After that, the display cases on the kitchen counter in my house grew in number and variety. After only a month and a half of training with a coach, my value on the market shot up. I invested in Thai pyrotechnics and started smoking $245 cigars. They were splendid.

Then I got myself a scalp. The Coahuila State Journalism Prize. My free pass: Prolific-plus. A *grupera* hit. A blend of Lidia Ávila and Martha Villalobos, the naughtiest, most savage, and bloodiest of the lesbian wrestlers in the porno industry.

The second prized mask I earned for myself was a scholarship from the Coahuila State Foundation for Afternoon Sewing and Arts Research. The project was the writing of a complete essay, the definitive book that would explain the relationship between my theoretical concepts about comeback wrestling, architorture, and electronic music at ranch weddings.

I made my final preparations the weekend the silver dwarf returned. It was at the French Alliance gallery. I called the exhibition *To Die in the Desert*. The press indulged me. According to the malicious gossips, the coverage was generous. But that's a lie. The press merely recognized my talent. The phrase for which they most detested me came from Ignacio Echevarría in *El País*: Menace Jr., the hip-hop empire's absolute magnate.

I freaked out that masked dwarf. Before he'd gone on tour, I was just a little unrefined brown sugar cube, but now I was a motorized mafioso terrorist. He'd need something a little more dangerous than a whip and a chair to avoid getting his little pocket trumpet of a head popped off.

Certain celebrity weddings had recently taken over the entertainment media and established an overwhelming tedium. They sold the fight as a vile mise-en-scène to a network that decided to hit its competition in the balls by broadcasting it via an open channel. No pay-per-view here.

The spectacle was called The Cursed Spring. The arena was packed. Yuri's voice got lost on home theater speakers among the barking vendors and the famished crowd, delirious and drunk. Beerpop. Noxious lunches. Gorditas with cholera.

First up on the widescreen was Santo's Son. His mentor was El Solitario. Mine was mini Espectrito. I left the rudo dressing room saturated with smoke. I'd made an offer of three Pandora LPs I'd burned between convulsions, untranslatable chants, prayers from postcards picked up on the highway.

I went dressed as a Cartesian seminarist. As soon as the guy in charge of composing the soundtrack to reflect the wrestling audience's passions saw me take a step toward the ring, he put on a song by the great Sonora Dinamita:

Ae ae ae ae.
Ae ae.
Ae ae ae ae.
Ae ae.
Cry, heart, cry.
Cry, heart, cry.
Cry, heart, cry, 'cuz your Lagunero ain't coming back.

There'll be two or three takedowns with no time limits to win the national welterweight championship. From the extreme rudos, the pride of the Lagunero District, La Diva, also known as Menace Jr. From the technical team, The Silver Mask, also known as Santo's Son.

Your Lagunero's going, babe.
Going and not coming back.
Your Lagunero's going, babe.
Going and not coming back.

Before any sound was heard, before the bell rang, a boy came up to the ropes to take a photo with me and a very sexy lady came over to give me a kiss. The place was divided. The dwarf's popularity didn't convince the rowdy thugs in the nosebleed seats, those guys who were only familiar with mortadella for lunch.

As soon as the action started, I planted myself between the four posts, opened my Cowboy Bible and began to preach in Yoruba: Black tongue, son of Menace, cumbianchero. I had the crowd spellbound, they were with me: Kill him. Kill him, Menace Jr. The sermon continued:

Jesus gonna be here.
Gonna be here soon.
You gotta keep the devil
Way down in the hole.

I beat Santo's Son with three takedowns. They didn't disqualify his suicide block, or a single hold, or even his straddling me. Cowboy Bible and belt in hand, I filled the mic with my maniac street preacher voice: Hey you, dwarf, campy film star, I challenge you to a match, just mask versus mask, no referee. Just us. Whipping our leather, whipping our courage. The star of so many ridiculous scripts responded: I accept, Menace Jr. Next week, right here, just one takedown.

Thursday, a day of tributes for the illustrious sport in Gomitos, we received notice that we were banished from the Olímpico Laguna. The reason given was that the first-division crowds threw too much stuff into the field. It happens frequently in soccer. So the match would take place behind closed doors and be broadcast on a national network.

The arena was empty. Just the second-string sound engineers hanging around their systems. We went up to the ring at the same time. Each one took his position at his corner. Behind the turntables.

It wasn't a fun or dramatic match. My opponent wiped the floor with me. He was his father's son. His collection of European vinyl was his advantage. It was huge. Broad. More than 2,500 records ready to go and fill a whole night of raving.

I did my best to get the most out of what I had, but no matter what kind of juxtapositions or genre acrobatics I played or sampled, no matter my programming or effects, the dwarf and his skills totally outdid me. All his equipment was first-rate. The needles, the earphones: Everything was imported.

The sacrilege I'd committed two hours earlier of breaking dozens of records proved irrelevant. The Cowboy Bible didn't respond either. I tore at it, implored it, cursed it, and still failed.

I didn't wait for word from the authorities to take off my mask; I failed and did it myself in front of the cameras. I said my name, declared my profession as a sociologist, and handed the trophy over to the winner.

On my way to the rudo dressing room, I placed the Cowboy Bible on the third seat of the front row and walked away with the idea that I might challenge Santo's Son in about a month, mask versus hairpiece, in my hometown, in San Pedro, Bahía.

COOLER BURRITOS

LA CUAUHNÁUAC was the most famous bar in the district for three reasons: The first was the house's special brew, the second was the name, and the third was the burritos they sold outside.

1. The special brew was sotol cured with tarbush, mint, peppermint, guava, and pumpkin seeds.

2. Its name came from the mythical sunken city.

3. And the burritos were made from machaca. A basic diet.

Of all the bars downtown, La Cuauhnáuac had the distinction of having among its clientele a drunkard who had established the record for imbibing the most cups of sotol in a single sitting: eighteen. Double shots. The indisputable ace, who had held the championship belt for two consecutive years, was The Cowboy Bible, a burrito vendor.

What made the brew so good was that it lost all its coarseness after it was cured. The guava gave it a killer taste. When people tried it they immediately loved the flavor. It went down smoothly. Three minutes later they asked for a second round, and six shots later they left on their hands and knees.

The brew became a big hit. A reporter for *El Norte*, while investigating an article about public transportation, became curious when she saw so many people congregating around the joint. Her reportorial instinct suggested scandal, yellow journalism, but when she went in she suffered the disappointment of finding personable treatment and a friendly environment.

The bartender served her a single shot. She drank it cautiously, but the guava flavor eased her fear. She ordered another and another and another. After the fourth, she fell asleep at the bar. It was only five in the afternoon. When she awakened, her watch read twelve midnight. It took her a moment to come to and she decided her watch was broken. But no. Outside, the night confirmed that she was the broken one. The bar was still bubbling with activity. She was relieved to discover she had not been raped. And it wasn't as if the others there didn't want to: The place was jammed with exactly the kind of sexually repressed perverts typical of a place that sold five-peso drinks, but they were all afraid of the bartender. Though not exactly the bartender, but the machete he had behind the bar. The guy in charge of the brothel hated it when they bothered his clients and, besides, he was a ladies' man, always ready to defend the femmes, whether they were fatales or not. The reporter ordered another sotol, pulled a notebook out of her purse and began taking notes.

The next day, there was an article in *El Norte*'s center spread. La Cuauhnáuac took up an entire page. The article attracted a new clientele. Among these were drinking aficionados, aspiring intellectuals, alcoholic college students, and an infinite number of weird and lazy self-taught trumpet players.

When all the other bars in the area that sold sotol saw this new popularity, they imitated La Cuauhnáuac's style of curing it, but not one was able to copy the recipe precisely. The ingredients were the same, but as in all things gourmet, the ultimate success was attributed to the bartender's masturbating hand.

All that rock and roll didn't last long. In less than six months, La Cuauhnáuac had stopped placing on the fashion lists. There was still a considerable crowd, but gone were the characters who had shown up during the apogee of its popularity and given the bar that trendy touch. A place free of prejudice. Showbizzy.

In order to keep the bar's popularity from fading, the bartender reached out to the girl reporter and asked a favor: to save the bar from anonymity by creating the first La Cuauhnáuac contest. It was a competition to see who could drink the most cups of sotol in a single sitting. They established three prizes. The first was five thousand pesos, the second three thousand, and the third two thousand.

The announcement attracted the attention of everyone that could still be seduced by that kind of folklore. Twenty-three contestants signed up, but the competition didn't last more than a half-hour. With a total of eighteen double shots, and without vomiting, The Cowboy Bible took first place.

The following year, during the second annual contest, The Cowboy Bible won again. He didn't need to repeat the record, because his closest rival had lost consciousness at the thirteenth cup. On the fourteenth, The Cowboy Bible paused and toasted with a beer.

In its third year, the contest got a little darker. The bars in the area had suffered a downturn, and some had closed. The more stubborn ones had used the contest as a betting game. At the beginning, in the second year of the competition, the bets had been between five and ten thousand pesos, but things got out of control when the local mafia got involved in the business. Bored with boxing, underground dogfights, and roulette, they found out about this peculiar contest and moved a certain percentage of their winnings to target sotol, their new blood.

For the third edition of the contest, the cash awards increased. First place was now ten thousand pesos, second was five, and third was three. Expectations also grew. The enthusiastic reporter promoted the spectacle, and they now anticipated about two thousand curiosity seekers. Three months ahead of time, they had to draw up a VIP list. The bar only had a capacity of sixty.

Plans began to spring up with the spontaneity that money allows. San Pedro, a capo and the biggest and heaviest of the drug barons on the scene, planned to take over the bar in order to manage the bets. It wouldn't take much effort to take over the place. He had the money to buy it, and if the owner refused to sell it, he could kill him, make him disappear. Later, he decided against it. He preferred the actual competition.

The fight for the money was set. Don Lucha Libre was the cash cow. He was the cocaine monster on the east side of the city. He controlled part of downtown, managed the bets, and kept the balance in his favor. The Cowboy Bible was part of his cartel. He was his pet.

Everybody knew The Cowboy Bible was unbeatable in any duel that involved swigging the special brew, but that did not affect the contest's immense popularity. A skillful mouth-to-mouth campaign had it that San Pedro would provide a worthy rival, a steely trueblood.

But that was a lie. He was simply feeling them out. San Pedro wanted to top Don Lucha Libre, but he knew that fighting in the bar was out of the question. The moment he went after any of the event's central figures, everything would fall apart. The bettors would disappear, and there would be no profits that year, no luck. Thus the bluff, the distraction.

The Cowboy Bible was at his peak as an inebriant. His ability to hold his liquor was a matter of record. He'd begun to drink at fourteen, and his talent had never diminished. No one could understand how he'd developed such a capacity. Two months before the contest he decided to have a trial run. There was no distinction between the first and the twelfth glass. He was tipping his fourteenth when the bartender (also his manager) stopped him. Stop, he said. That's enough. Take a shower. The test suggested that on a good afternoon The Cowboy Bible could put away twenty or thirty double shots.

San Pedro wanted very much to be the new gambling marquis. He had everything he needed for the role: contacts in the judiciary, a wide-tire truck in the preferred baroque style of the drug barons, and credit in Sinaloa. The only thing stopping him was Don Lucha Libre. The aging minotaur had years in the business, and it would not be easy to take over the labyrinth built on the downtown streets by his pushers.

In order to become the new Christopher Columbus of wholesale distribution and blind weigh-in, San Pedro planned to bribe one of Don Lucha Libre's intimates. The list of untouchables included the bartender and, obviously, the aspirant to the title. The only available target was Sussy, The Cowboy Bible's wife. With great sacrifice, the woman made burritos so that her husband could go against God and make a living as a drunk. San Pedro had only one card, and he played it.

As it turned out, Sussy was easy. She hated her husband's celebrity. She angrily remembered when they had begun the burrito business together. The Cowboy Bible was a natural-born drinker. She'd chosen to put up with the situation and didn't care one bit that he was an alcoholic. She trusted their profits could support his pastime. They never did too badly, as burritos were better than tamales and less hassle. Their first day, they got up early. Sussy prepared the stew, and he went to get a cooler. It was blue. Brand name Iglú. It had enough room for two hundred burritos wrapped in parchment paper.

The Cowboy Bible had known the bartender at La Cuauhnáuac since infancy; they'd been in elementary school and done military service together. When the future champion found out his buddy had a dive, he became a star client. Then the bartender gave him a chance to set up outside and sell his burritos. From the very first night on, the drunks would empty the cooler.

But their apparent prosperity was deceiving. About half their profits would disappear when they paid the tab The Cowboy Bible ran up at the bar. He was good at fueling up. When he got famous, he refused to help make the burritos. Sussy had made a last-ditch effort to save him from such a lack of productivity, but it was useless. The Cowboy Bible had become an underground rock star and spent all day at La Cuauhnáuac with a beer in one hand, wearing dark glasses, long hair, a two-week-old beard, sandals, and shorts.

When San Pedro approached Sussy, she turned out to be an excellent businesswoman and not much of a comfort to her husband. She was willing to cooperate but wanted a percentage of the pot—not just a generous cut, but the principal cut. San Pedro's response was immediate: No way. Not only would he deny her such a sum, but he also refused to let her bet. That turf was reserved for the heaviest people; not even the nasty narco-retailers were allowed to bet. Only the heaviest heavies, and maybe one or two eccentrics who had a green light to bring trailers over the border, were on the list. To add a stranger would provoke suspicion. The cook would surely know that such an ingredient could ruin the stew.

Sussy told San Pedro to stop pretending, that he could include her at the betting tables. If you want to win, set me up. It was an insinuation, an insult directed at the drug baron. But he wasn't bothered. He remembered the rules of the underworld: No sympathy for the devil. They closed the deal—a slot at the third table. They'd unleashed the dog. Sussy had committed herself to eliminating her husband. That poor sucker wouldn't even be able to get up the day of the contest.

At the start of the year, the bartender suggested The Cowboy Bible go on a diet, a safeguard for his stomach. Never. The Cowboy Bible wouldn't take any precautions. Men didn't do that. For three years, he had been nourished on machaca burritos and would not modify his regimen. Sussy's seasoning had made him what he was. The burritos were his Special K.

The burritos' fame was almost as great as that of La Cuauhnáuac. They were known throughout the western side of the city. And as usually happens, they had been given the chance to expand their business. The first big order came from a young PAN loyalist who thought it would be cool to serve Sussy's ice cooler burritos on her birthday.

Sussy had not counted on anyone to help her. The Cowboy Bible had said he would, but then refused: I'm hungover, *vieja*. You go at it, and if you manage to stay up all night, you'll finish them. Whether more or fewer burritos, Sussy took care of the orders. In the meantime, The Cowboy Bible spent each afternoon shadowboxing at La Cuauhnáuac. The contest date was nearing. Rumors about an opponent who was up to snuff meant he had to increase his training.

In the next two weeks, the master burrito micro-industry went off the charts. The birthday girl told all her friends that the burritos from La Cuauhnáuac were fantastic. In order to keep up with trends, several very chic girls from her school asked their daddies for burrito parties. I can make them for you, one mother told her daughter. No, absolutely not. But it's no big deal, *hija*. No, mama, they have to be street burritos. Do you understand?

The list of orders grew and Sussy could not keep up by herself. A week from the contest, the publicity campaign ramped up. The drug baron wanted his own Las Vegas at the corner of Madero and Villagrán, and he invested even more in propaganda. The Cowboy Bible dedicated the following week to finishing his training on the hill at La Campana.

San Pedro began to pressure Sussy, because The Cowboy Bible had not interrupted his training. It was looking like he would reign again as the idol of the gutless, the consul of the lumpen-depraved, the idiot drinker who would cost San Pedro thousands of pesos. It's time to force a change, he said. We can't lose.

Sussy wasn't sure she'd be able to keep up her end of the deal. Preparing the burritos exhausted her, left her too wasted to plan the conspiracy they needed to perpetrate against the father of her non-existent children. She didn't know what to do to keep her *viejo* from showing up at the contest.

But then The Cowboy Bible returned from La Campana in a physical condition that assured their victory. Don Lucha Libre wanted to underwrite a trip for him to Liberia so that he wouldn't turn into a pimp, but they reconsidered, since his opponent had surely not even arrived in Villa Juárez to prepare himself. With a little visit to the Formula 1 spa, surely The Cowboy Bible's motor would be able to get some rest.

Finally the day of the contest arrived. The excitement spread all over the city's downtown. At ten in the morning, a parade officially kicked off the madness. A caravan sponsored by Coca-Cola led the way, polar bears included. Those in charge of logistics warned the narco that he'd look foolish. We don't give a damn, we have more than enough bears, they taunted. For them, it was Christmas and New Year's all year long. Besides, how would we be noticed without these red trucks? When have people not turned around to look at the colored lights on the damn trucks, soda cans painted on the sides?

At noon, a betting festival commenced at the Plaza de Armas. There was a food court, free sotol, and music by *cumbia* and norteño groups. At six in the afternoon, the show ended with Valentín Elizalde. People were already drunk and crazy, and everybody, including the street vendors from Oaxaca, had gathered in front of La Cuauhnáuac. As in every gala, there was a red carpet. The star hosting the event was the editor of the music magazine *Furia*. Carmen Salinas and the singer from Nilo Gallardo's band, Mocorito, were among the distinguished guests. Also present were representatives from Noni Juice of Mexico, the technical director from Santos Laguna, and local superstar Wendolí, since phased out from the first generation of *La Academia*.

The public was yearning to see the masked men die onstage. The rapper Chico Ché's famous rhymes could be heard coming from the speakers: El Santo, El Cavernario, Blue Demon, y El Bulldog. Beer spewed as if in an epiphany had by any Irishman with glaucoma.

There were thirty-two contestants. Two resigned when they realized there was no swimsuit competition. They all took their places. The Cowboy Bible's rival behaved like an anxious swimmer, the kind who's so nervous he dives in before the starting shot. The only person missing was the champion, who also had the record for the slowest speed onto the track. A world record and a Gatorade-ad image. The people were behind him. He had every right to be brazen; it's not every day you can write an exemplary novel.

A limousine waited outside The Cowboy Bible's house, the motor running. Inside, on his knees, looking very cowboyish in a chapel improvised Malverde-style, the champion prayed. He dedicated the fight to Saint Jude. In song, he asked that if he did not come back alive, his family be taken care of.

Solemnly, he got up and made his way to his dressing room. He put on his cowboy suit and helmet, and went into the kitchen. Before each bout, he engaged in the ceremonious act of eating cooler burritos. He had to eat something greasy in order to deal with the brew. Sussy didn't serve him from the stew in the pot. Instead, she pulled four pork burritos from her socks that she had spoiled earlier that day. She stripped them of their wrapping and threw them on the fire. Once warmed, she wrapped them in napkins, like astronaut food, and handed them to The Cowboy Bible, burrito master. He packed them up. The underworld needed entertainment. Fresh meat. It didn't matter if it was sirloin steak or dried beef. Sussy didn't want to go with him. She refused to get in the limousine. How can I possibly go dressed like this? Besides, I have to go take an order to some lady's house so her little princess won't cause a scene in the middle of her *quinceañera*.

On his way to the duel, the burritos began to have an effect on The Cowboy Bible. Digestion was not imperative. The limousine pulled to the side, and the champion exploded. Instead of flour and pork, it looked like he'd been stuffed with pig's feet stew. It hurt so much, it felt as if the pig's entire foot—hairy and chewed up and without a pedicure—had come up his throat.

An impatient Don Lucha Libre dialed the limousine's number: Goddamn it, you sons of bitches, where are you, why the hell aren't you here? The driver, also The Cowboy Bible's bodyguard, answered, bewildered, The Kid has fallen apart, boss, he's vomiting. It can't be. Fucking Christ. Take him home. I'm on my way. Don't tell anyone.

The winner of the competition to see who could lift more rolls of Bimbo bread with one finger walked inside trembling. He was in a cold sweat. A fever of a hundred and four degrees was burning his guts. He threw himself into bed.

Once things were in motion, Sussy put on the new dress San Pedro had sent her. The six ice coolers fit in the taxi. The trip cost fifty pesos. She finished her task, and the lady of the house complimented her on her evening dress: How handsome, Susanita. She left with money in hand. She was looking really good; she looked like a narco's woman.

She took another taxi to La Cuauhnáuac. The riot of the party could be heard four blocks away. Big rigs—brand name: Truckalicious—formed a long line of this year's models as if in a showroom. Cars kept coming, and people kept jamming the streets. It was a herd of groupies. They came down from the trees, up from the gutter, and out from under rocks.

Security was thick, lots of former-drivers-turned-badass-bodyguards. It took Sussy ten minutes to reach the line separating the chosen from the undesirable. It was hard to tell which performance on which side of the line was more grotesque.

Sussy's name wasn't on the list. Like my mother told me, never trust a narco and even less one who had glass balls as a kid. And if her name wasn't on the invite list, there was even less chance it'd be on the bettors list. Damn life, damn misery.

She hung around outside the bar for half an hour. The bartender looked out the door because he'd been accused of cheating. He'd given courtesy passes and sold memberships without permission from the narco bureaucracy. He saw Sussy and yelled at her: Hey you, what the fuck are you doing here? Get in the kitchen, we don't have enough people to attend to our guests. And if you're ever late again, I'll kill you. Sussy started to head inside, but one of the guards stopped her. The boss had sent orders that she not go in. The bartender screamed at the guard that if she couldn't come in he should wait tables himself. The other guard intervened: Let her go in. Mind your own business. You're nobody here, and she's not coming in. Yes, come on in. C'mon, c'mon, hurry up. But in spite of the tussle, she never got in.

Inside, the booing and shouting was unstoppable. The Cowboy Bible was nowhere to be seen. San Pedro's smile invited Don Lucha Libre's suspicions. From the Stern-brand speakers came the announcement that the champion was trapped in a traffic jam. What a joke! A traffic jam in a town that small? He would be there any moment. In the meantime, let's serve dinner. San Pedro didn't protest. He could snatch up his money and go, but he wanted to see how far the show would go. In any case, he didn't care about the money; the juicy part of the deal was that he'd get complete control of all of the drug-distribution points downtown.

The Cowboy Bible arrived with the championship belt held high and a green face. There was no fight in him. He cheapened the battle by only being able to hold down five cups of the brew. A new champion and a new distributor had stolen the spotlight. Don Lucha Libre was a good loser; he handed the business to San Pedro, and they continued drinking. Nobody left the bar. Los Capi were about to play.

The limo driver approached Don Lucha Libre and let him know Sussy was outside. He gave him the lowdown: His Cowboy Bible had been poisoned. Without moving from his privileged seat, Don Lucha Libre pulled out his pistol and killed San Pedro with one shot. That single shot was all it took to spark the shootout that ended the lives of all those present, including the new monarch and The Cowboy Bible.

The following day's newspaper had headlines across eight columns. There had been a great settling of scores in the world of organized crime. Extrafifí Agency, Thursday, December 27th: At five in the morning yesterday, police officers as well as officers from alcohol control, entered La Cuauhnáuac with the intention of closing it for its failure to observe blue laws. Instead, they found everyone inside had been killed, including the heads of the local drug underworld.

Sussy never again mentioned La Cuauhnáuac or the deaths or anything. The following week, she began from scratch once more outside the bar, but she couldn't sell a single burrito. One night as she was putting away her things, a man came up and asked if she knew where he could get some coke. No. I don't know. Damn it, said the *cholo*, I'm going fucking cold turkey. Aren't there any narcos left in this city? No. There aren't any anymore, young man. Here, buy one of my burritos. No. Fuck that burrito. What I need is to get some coke. I already told you, young man. There are no more narcos. There are no more narcos. It's better if you just buy one of my burritos. C'mon, don't be a bad guy. I have some machaca burritos.

NON-FICTION

REISSUE OF THE ORIGINAL FACSIMILE OF THE REMASTERED COUNTRY BIBLE'S BACK COVER*

For Fernando del Paso

Beauty she is scarred into man's soul,
A flower attracting lust, vice, and sin,
A vine that can strangle life from a tree,
Carrion, surrounding, picking on leaves

SHE IS SUFFERING,
MANIC STREET PREACHERS

---

* a.k.a. The Western Bible.

A) RISE AND SHINE

THE SCIENCE OF PIRACY was a ghost that had always lived in The Country Bible's heart. Ever since she was a kid, riding around on a *gallito* in this trashy town. Home to bootlegging, to contraband, to treason imported from all over, from Sevastopol, Anchorage, Cardiff.

Ever since she bought her ticket to this world (at Ticketmaster), one of the young Country Bible's better features was her attachment to tradition. Since she herself was a product of the Tetra Pak generation, she was determined to pay tribute to the Old School. That was, in fact, our heroine's specialty: to conduct herself in the old ways.

We didn't understand why she felt indebted to the Old Guard. It didn't really come naturally. Even her parents, on a few drunken occasions (with national or imported brews), considered baptizing her Moderna Tenenbaum. They also considered Poliforma Multiforme, but in the end settled on The Country Bible, in honor of the socio-delic breakfast.

The Country Bible descended from a long line of fried-chicken vendors. Most recently, her grandfather, father, and siblings wore the obligatory apron at Henry's Chicken. Since her dreams of travel were in check, she decided to place them alongside her aspirations to piracy and began to go to school.

The line that divides the client from the employer does not make them different from one another. The person who clerks at a record store, the guy who polarizes the windshield, and the server at the chicken stand are all spineless simpletons, incapable of rebelling.

Here's the lowdown on The Country Bible: One of the reasons she stepped out from behind the counter was that her family, from the moment fast food came to the civilized world, had always been employed at Henry's Chicken. Not a single relative, not even her grandfather, who, according to family lore, had been the most prosperous in their lineage, had ever managed to own one of the chain stores. Not one sad little franchise had ever come within reach of any of them.

So began the militancy, the dissidence of The Country Bible. I don't think anybody indoctrinated her, or even invited her; she made her own decision to join the Communist Youth, with the same enthusiasm an adolescent has when they join a rock band. Influenced by what was trendy, she adopted the look of a typical UNAM student. When she wasn't working, and in order to complete her militant presentation, she dove into required readings every time she bit down on an apple. She transformed herself into an encyclopedia of Latin American folklore. She furnished her room with Willem de Kooning posters and built a piracy laboratory, equipped with a tower that could burn twelve records at once and was also multifunctional: It could photocopy covers and had an inscription device to make copies of the text.

As a practitioner of piracy, The Country Bible tried to live covertly, like an infiltrator. She swung between the cool underground flavor of the marmalade of torture so that she could dedicate herself fully to the proletarian struggle, to her top spot serving breaded potatoes at the chicken joint. She stayed at Henry's Chicken because she didn't want to turn her back on tradition. But her revolutionary attitude began to cause her typical teenage problems.

The first sign of trouble came at work. Anxiety is expressed in three basic ways: random laughter, sweaty palms, and involuntary and inevitably absurd behavior. One boring afternoon at the chicken joint, The Country Bible was afflicted by the third kind. It was one of those days merchants call slow. At four in the afternoon, as a distraction, and with the wisdom of an indelible marker, she wrote nicknames for all the employees, manager included, on the workers' punch cards.

The general discontent was over the top. The names themselves didn't bother the employees; it was that they didn't understand them. If only she'd written sly stuff like The Booger, The Flying Chimijuil, or The Pincher, then they would have tolerated it. Instead she designated the workers with names beloved to her leftist soul: Cienfuegos, John Lennon, Heberto Castillo, Lenin. Ever since The Country Bible had begun to express herself through protest songs, everybody said that she was distancing herself from the streets of the barrio. Every day she identified more with the Great Latin American Social Breach. But what neither the rechristened employees nor The Country Bible herself suspected was the split suffered by the fried-chicken vendor who would bring together the proletariat struggle and business interests in the events of October 2nd.

The following day, she received a notice from management. The workers demanded the traitor be burned. But they didn't fire her. Because there was a superstition in the business that it was best to have at least one Country Bible at the counter to protect them from secondhand witchcraft. They suspended her for one week.

B) SUNNYSIDE UP

She took advantage of her free time, with masterful use of forceps, to strengthen her ties to the Communist Party. Piracy, like LSD at the very beginning, was legal until the lunatics at the CIA decided that it wasn't, that all those stoned adolescents shouldn't listen to Violeta Parra all the time. They launched an attack they could have called You-Will-Cry against everyone involved in commercial piracy. So The Country Bible's hobby changed. It transformed into something along the lines of Shit, dude, I didn't bring the Serrat, but on this CD I have a Word version of the Communist Manifesto.

She became a wizard in everything that had to do with PCs and information. She was in charge of distributing copies of the CDs with instructions for the movement. From her post in the historic district, she would distribute records with covers that featured Paulina Rubio, El Viejo

Paulino, Alejandra Guzmán, Polo Polo. In truth, they did not contain the hits of the day, nor poems recited by Paco Stanley, but rather specifications for a demonstration by the merchants from the Plaza de las Tres Culturas that would take place October 2nd.

The conflict had begun because of an uproar among peddlers. At the time, a kind of street market had grown around the merchants, but everyone gathered there had been rudely kept down by the cops. Sick of the abuse and ready for a fight with the Díaz Ordaz government, the merchants organized and subscribed to the PC.

During a march on August 31st, TV cameras captured a dramatic moment: A young woman wearing a chicken-vendor uniform joined the protest. The young woman was The Country Bible herself, who had decided to wear her yellow suit, fuck people's retinas. Her only other option was to have gone as Chabuca Granda.

This would change the direction the festivities would take. From the burning of the Judas figure, to the costumes worn decades later in gay pride marches, to the celebration of goals scored on the field—every apotheosis would be affected, on its outside, at its core, and in all the places where anti-wrinkle cream is effective, by The Country

Bible's proposed innovations on that historic date. The Díaz Ordaz government, which had always looked upon the merchants with red-rimmed eyes, now rushed to support them, terrified of the idea that the merchants could affect the buildup to the next Olympic Games.

Life went on like a giant jar of horchata. In Tlatelolco on October 2nd the merchants and the army faced off. The events created a deep black hole in the history of Mexico. A myth grew about thousands dead and disappeared. The officials claimed the merchants had begun the shooting. It was whispered that a special group of peddlers, the Olympic Battalion, had infiltrated the soldiers and begun firing. That was when those up front let themselves go.

The army was now prepared to confront the merchants, whose weapons were like water pistols in comparison to those of their opponents. After the massacre, nonstop butchering was visited on the survivors. The merchants tried to run and hide in the apartments around Tlatelolco and its surroundings; they looked everywhere for hiding places, even under the last metro ticket, but it was useless. Hundreds were captured. Some were tortured, and others disappeared. It was all fucked up.

That was the hell preceding the 1968 Olympic Games. The wound has remained open in this country's memory to this day. In the following decades, the massacre would inspire innumerable songs, novels, movements, and films. Monuments, statues, and monoliths were erected, plazas and streets named in honor of the fallen.

C) MORNING GLORY

The grievances against the government took a toll on its authority. Once the smoke of the massacre cleared, the party in power, with help from the FBI, proposed to capture the movement leadership and released a list with the names and photographs of those implicated. The Country Bible was among them. The star of the moment wore a flower costume in the photograph. It looked like a joke. We didn't know if they were looking for a possible political prisoner or Peter Gabriel during his Genesis days. But the government found it impossible to find a photo in which she wasn't dressed as some character. In the photo from her primary school graduation, she wore a Menace Jr. wrestling mask. In the one from high school, she was dressed as the old man from *The Lamb Lies Down on Broadway*.

The people were offended: How is it possible that the president would send soldiers, unprepared, without arms, to combat those bastards sent by the Tepito Merchants?

Every time something politically inconvenient comes up, the government creates a distraction. A few months before the Olympic Games, so that the people would forget the Jalisco-style massacre, Díaz Ordaz ordered Channel Eleven to create a reality show. Even though it was illegal, piracy had become fashionable, so it therefore became the theme of the show. The format was designed to reward the contestant who managed to copy the most records in a certain period of time. They settled on this because they'd run out of other ideas. There were already reality shows about people wrestling cows, about hip-hop stars, about wrestlers, about beauties and nerds, even one about aspiring comics.

With this move, Díaz Ordaz told his government secretary, Luis Echeverría, we'll capture those involved in the pirating sector. Oh, yes, sir, said the secretary, but what about the smugglers, those who sell stolen auto parts, the ranch hands? Don't get ahead of yourself, my dear right-hand man, everyone will get what they deserve. You just watch me play politics. These ones must fall first because they're the biggest pinkos. In any case, the high command assures me that The Country Bible, a dangerous terrorist who leads the movement, will sign up for the contest.

The government wasn't too far off base. To keep her head down for a while, The Country Bible tried out for the cast of *The Pirate Academy* and was accepted. Her popularity as a PC pirate member would give her away during the contest. She'd be arrested before the finale.

The Country Bible knew they were looking for her and, as a counterintelligence measure to avoid being recognized, she showed up dressed as a wrestler. Menace Jr., no less.

She wore a mask with the following features:

STATUS: She has not lost the mask.

MATERIAL: Dublin.

DESIGN: One of the most minimalist masks in wrestling, it has a seriousness that elevates it practically to elegance. All black, this mask's only aesthetic element is the silver border

around the eyes, nose, and mouth. An engraved white cross adorns the forehead.
OBSERVATIONS: Part of a great wrestling dynasty.
MANUFACTURER: Jesús Andrade.

So as not to drag out the programming, the results were posted every day at eight o'clock on Channel Eleven on the *El Recreo Show*. The Country Bible made the finals thanks to the calls from the public, who saved her three times when she was nominated for expulsion.

The finale was broadcast from the Auditorio Nacional. The host, Raquel Bigorra, stirred up the audience, encouraging them to call call call right now and vote for their favorite. Menace Jr. was second out of the four candidates. The difference between the two top slots was small. The testosterone emitting from The Country Bible's rival kept all the quinceañeras dialing. But Menace Jr. wanted the top prize. Fifty thousand pesos and a trip to Puerto Vallarta, all expenses paid. The package included three days and two nights in a suite for two at the Playa Hotel, but let's get back to you, Raquel, to see how the voting is going:

Right now, there are 12,543 calls for Menace Jr. and 12,856 for Erasmo. A reminder that there are only twenty minutes left to vote, then we'll stop the count. Our next participant is a native of San Pedro Rico. This is Menace Jr.'s last chance to convince the judges. Proceed.

To surprise the judges, The Country Bible ascended the stage wearing an outfit over her wrestling costume. She was disguised as Demis Roussos over her Country Bible Junior costume. While she burned CDs as fast as her prosthetic belly and beard would allow, the hits played in the background: Goodbye, my love, goodbye. The phones wouldn't stop, and Menace Jr. came in first place. She'd won the third round.

A week later, the Mexican Federation of Reality Shows, presided over by Decio de María, voided the prize, fined Channel Eleven, and banned them from producing reality shows for an entire year. The argument was that Menace Jr., who'd never removed the mask, had turned out positive on the doping tests, with her blood rich in Nandrolone; steroids had helped her win. They took the award away and canceled the trip. Something similar had happened at the Reality World Championships in Italy, but Mexico hadn't participated because of some *cachirules*.

Thirty years later, The Country Bible is still the glory of the neighborhood. She's never been caught. She still does interviews, and there's a new biopic about her that will premiere in the next few months. Around the same time, Echeverría will be coming up for trial. The files on the Tlatelolco massacre were reopened. It was finally revealed that it was he who gave the order to have the soldiers confront those merchant *cabrones*.

LIKE 'EM FAT

Very very fat
Fat fat
Superfat
Fat fat and tight

ORQUESTA MONDRAGÓN

A FAT GIRL. A fat girl. I needed a fat girl. Not to make tamales, nor to make her cry. I needed a fat girl to make love to her.

I'd heard thousands of stories at the bar. Legends, fantastic tales. I was particularly fascinated by the myths about men who slept with fat girls: Fat girls were said to rekindle their faith in love. The overweight woman was attributed prowess and sexual expertise that are not to be found in the rest of her gender. Because fatness presumes an aesthetic disadvantage, these fatties develop skills to compensate for what they lack and for their excessive roundness.

I had no way of knowing if this was true. I had never slept with a fat girl. I'm fat, but obese men don't enjoy the same reputation. We're known as terrible lovers. That's what they say at the bar. I don't know if that's true either. I've never had sex with a fat man.

I had never slept with a fat girl, but it wasn't because I discriminate. It's just that skinny girls drove me crazy. Their meatless little bones. Their little chicken legs, as if they had avian flu. They were my perdition for one single reason: They were cheap. The little birdies would just eat their birdseed—and so quietly! I dislike drunks and addicts. A woman who drinks more than you can lead you to ruin. That's what I was counseled at the bar. Whenever anybody on the street tried to come on to me saying stuff like, The greater the flesh, the greater the sin, I'd just start counting numbers.

I decided to try to find a heavyset woman because I couldn't have relations with my little wife. I didn't know a thing about fat girls. At the bar they said getting it on with one it was like getting lost in a gigantic plasma all night. I wasn't looking for a special fat girl. I'd be happy with anyone who could reawaken my faith in love.

I had stopped sleeping with my wife because she disobeyed me. It's curious. The fight started because I refused to take her to a dance where Valentín Elizalde was playing. I told her she couldn't go alone. She paid me no mind. She and her sister climbed into the Grand Marquis and left without my permission.

At the dance, she ran into the devil. The guy who asked her to dance was born with a goat's hoof and a rooster's foot. The place started to smell of smoke, and all hell broke loose. My wife turned up burned to a crisp in the Red Cross emergency room. It was even in the newspaper. I don't think the devil was on tour with Valentín. I wasn't there. Nonetheless, the guys at the bar assure me that's what happened. I'm the laughing stock of the neighborhood. And my wife believes they put the idea in my head. Everybody, including kids, now screams at me, The devil sucked off your wife, *güey*. It's as if you dropped a piece of candy on the ground and can't pick it up because it's stuck to the dirt. Everything for God, nothing for the devil, my wife reproached me, but I hadn't been able to find the sweetness in her body again.

Before I decided to try for the fat girl, there were others. But my game was off. I couldn't get it out of my head that if that guy hadn't turned out to be the devil, my wife would have ended up in bed with him. What good did it do me to throw myself at pound after pound of woman flesh, at the whole neighborhood, if I couldn't figure out how to touch my own?

Then I heard another guy at the bar say, That whore weighed two hundred kilos. She stunk so badly, she was disgusting. And in spite of that, I still climbed on her as if she was a pancake and squirted until I couldn't anymore. You have no idea. I recovered my faith in life. This was the final push to move me to try to win a fat girl's favors. It's easy, I told myself. The world is full of fat girls. But I was wrong. There were ten prospective fat girls. One overdosed on coke, and so there were nine. Another one got raped by some cripple, so then there were only eight. Et cetera.

Why don't you leave her? they asked me at the bar. Find someone else. So many hours on the stool made these drinkers think most men in my position would have gotten a separation. But I wasn't part of that proud brotherhood. I didn't dare leave my wife because I had already invested too much. One of my mother's recurrent complaints about me is that I'm like my grandmother, incapable of throwing anything away. I still have all the notebooks I used in elementary school, my toys, and the lottery numbers I bought from Simón Simonazo. I have a real talent for not getting rid of things.

The perfect fat girl. When I got tired of that bouquet of fatties, the idea of getting a specific fat girl began to tempt me. Who would be my chosen fat girl? Would it be one of the Ultrasonics or one of the Poquianchis? My love life's welfare depended on the flesh of a well-padded girl. Where would such a wonder be found? How deep would the ecstasy go?

In order to make my search more efficient, I put an ad in the newspaper: *Looking for fat girl. Looking for a domestic helper saddled with the yoke of obesity. My wife is very jealous. Don't even bother to present yourself if you're not aesthetically unfortunate*. But my ad was a failure. My fat girl remained out of reach. Hopeless, I took refuge in a concert by Buki, Jesus Christ to sentimental fat girls. That's where I learned my first lesson as a hunter of *chicharronería* customers: Fat girls are expensive. That sentimental prototype exceeded my budget.

Without actually thinking about it, my senses led me to the Olímpico Laguna, the wrestling arena with the greatest traditions here in San Pedrostuttgart. And that's where the perfect victim appeared. A fragile and defenseless nineteen-year-old fat girl. The lamb, no, excuse me, the cow who would free me from the sins of the world. I tell you, it wasn't premeditated. I'd just gone to enjoy the fights, and she came and sat down next to me, she just roundly settled beside me.

She was called The Western Bible. At first, I thought that she was pulling my leg. Later, that she was crazy. She swore the crazy ones were her parents and showed me her voter registration card. It was no joke. The Western Bible really was The Western Bible. She was one imposing heifer: tall, blond, and so plump. And she wasn't alone. She was with her son. I bought two beers and a Coca-Cola for the little calf. She told me they lived alone. She didn't know who her son's father was, and she had no intention of finding out. Her parents were in another house, in another city. It occurred to me they had fled from her. That they had left her the house and were supporting her at a distance, so long as they didn't have to deal with her. The story was perhaps a bit fantastic, like the ones from the bar. Trying to have a romance with a fat girl was making me paranoid. Maybe they just lived apart because of work. But why didn't they take her with them?

From the very beginning of the show, I began asking myself how I was going to approach this young, fat, blond single mother. How was I going to insinuate to this robust female that I needed her vigor to reignite a carnal desire for my wife? Would I dare to shamelessly ask for her ass? Would I wait for her to offer it in some natural way? Would I appeal to her sense of single motherhood? To a sense of necessary sluttishness given her situation?

I couldn't take any chances. I decided to rely on my slyer aspects. I ordered two more beers and a mortadella plate for the boy. No chilies. I bought him a Menace Jr. mask and, before the second fight had begun, he climbed up into the ring. The Western Bible focused on her son's evolution in the wrestling ring as she drank her Victoria beer. She was distracted. Without hesitating, I took her hand and placed it on my fly. She did not complain, but retrieved her hand. Since she didn't turn to look, I took her hand again and placed it on myself, and she took it back again. I ordered two more beers, and we continued with that same routine throughout the show, me insisting she put her hand on my less noble parts and her refusing to do so, until the second takedown during the last fight, when The Western Bible let her hand rest on my fly. The circle had been completed. I would know the indulgent love secrets of a fat girl's spacious bed.

As we were leaving the arena, The Western Bible stopped cold. If only she would allow me to explore her and discover for myself the promising pleasures inherent in excessive adiposity. She agreed, but only after we were certain her boy was asleep. It would be inconvenient if he saw me; that's how it is with fatherless children. Unfortunately, every time somebody decides to screw their mothers, they develop a resistance to sleep.

So while the boy fell asleep, I walked a few blocks, bought some condoms, and, bored, finally, although reluctantly, went into a bar. I considered leaving, forgetting everything, and just going home. But I couldn't. In some way, The Western Bible was already mine. I'd already spent a fortune on our beers. I didn't want to later regret having passed up the opportunity.

My cellphone rang, and it was her. It took two hours for the little calf's battery to run out. During that time,

The Western Bible had been hitting the whiskey. She'd taken some good hits. Like a trucker. When I got there, she'd already finished one bottle and had a good start on a second. She offered me a drink, but I said no. She got pissy. She tried to hit me in the mouth and splashed my shirt. I had a momentary doubt but decided I had things under control. Anyway, if the fat girl became insufferable, I could fix everything by slapping her around, she might even like it. Maybe she'd like it and beg me for more.

It'd be better if you took a bath, I told her. She came out covered in powder. She looked like a giant, overactive French loaf. I've always wanted to fuck in my parents' bed, she said, and then crossed the backyard completely nude, the bottle in one hand and a CD in the other. Oh, this is going to get bad, I thought when I saw the king-size bed. I turned on a porn channel, put on the CD, and undressed. We hadn't even gotten to the second song when I realized The Western Bible was drunk out of her mind. No, not out of it, but blind drunk.

Grotesquely erotic, she spread out on the mattress and began to suck me off. My god, she was horrible. She choked. My dick was getting red. Twice I told her to leave it alone. You don't know what you're doing, I told her. You don't know how to suck. But she was determined to show me otherwise and she was hurting me. Hold on, hold on, I finally said. I'm really hot and I want to stick it in you. I screamed, pretending to be on the verge and managing to get away from her teeth. But she didn't give me a chance to do anything, quickly throwing herself on top of me. *Puta madre*, that fat girl weighed a ton, she completely pinned me. We began to push and pull, and I thought I would asphyxiate under her mass. It was frustrating. I immediately thought of my wife. Poor woman. She must feel the same thing when I'm on top. It must have taken so much sacrifice and devotion for her to tolerate my corpulence on her rickety little body.

The Western Bible stopped the pulling and pushing. I love that song, she said and got off the king-size bed to play it again. On her way to the stereo, she staggered, crashed against the dresser, and fell to the floor. I helped her up, and we continued with the penetration. I still had not experienced the divine loving grace of fatness when she again stopped to play the song over. Holy fuck, I shouted. Why don't you just let it play? Concentrate.

Well, no, we'll hear it a third time. And don't scream at me, *pendejo*.

She wanted to climb on me again, but it was useless. I couldn't take any more. My dick had deflated. We'll stop here, I said, but she would not give up. She insisted on continuing. And to motivate me, she tried to suck me off again. Listen, *puta*, I agree that fellatio is an art, but it is not impossible for a mortal to do it decently, I said. Haven't you ever eaten a popsicle? I asked her. It's not science. It's like sucking a Tootsie Pop. She changed tactics and got worse. Stop, stop, I shouted. I know what I'm doing, I know what I'm doing, she said in her defense, and because she was talking with her mouth full, she bit me. She refused to release me. To loosen her grip I slapped her. Then two more times, each time angrier than the other. She got up and hit me. I grabbed her and, with some effort, got her off me. I started to get dressed. She left the room, nude, with the bottle of whiskey in her hand.

When I got to the door, the fat girl came up to me. Don't leave, *cabrón*. You've exhausted me, you fucking greaseball. You're like all the others, you think I'm crazy. You're like my parents.

Just what I needed, puta, the venting. I'm leaving, I said again, but I couldn't open the door. It had a double lock.

It needed a key. Give me the fucking key, I screamed. She didn't want to give it up. Where is it?

Why don't you understand? she began pleading. Don't you understand? She poked my temples with her fingers and kept saying, I'm fine. This is normal, I just get depressed because I used to take drugs.

Stop, stop, I said. That's not my fault. The key.

It's not my fault I don't have friends. I'm normal, normal, but everybody wants to drive me crazy. You want to drive me crazy, she barked, and then came at me. I avoided her fist, but she wouldn't stop, so I finally punched her in the face with a closed fist.

Now in control and more eloquent, I demanded the key. The Western Bible was strewn on the floor. The key, *chingada madre*, or do you want another? Weak, she got up and said, You want your key? I'll get your damn key, and she disappeared. I saw the bottle of whiskey and shoved it under my jacket. I would get drunk to forget this terrible moment. The Western Bible came back and, to make me turn towards her, she said, Here's your key, *culero*. She was pointing a gun at me. I felt the blood drain out of me. It's possible it wasn't loaded, and she was pointing it just to get my attention, but I wasn't interested in finding out. I didn't dare wrestle this drunken mastodon for a gun at three in the morning. The little calf was still not awake. But with so much noise, he should have already been out of bed. If the boy could see us, The Western Bible would calm down and I could probably climb up the roof.

Nobody hits me, *hijo de chingada*. Nobody drives me crazy. I couldn't do or say anything. I was shitting my pants. She could easily misfire. I thought about screaming, crying for help, but that was ridiculous. Besides, nobody was going to get out of bed to save an imbecile like me. Fortunately, the little calf began to cry and The Western Bible took off to console him. I immediately started looking for the keys. They were hanging from a wooden cross in the kitchen. I took another moment to reach into her purse on top of the refrigerator and grab as much as I had spent on the two of them at the fights, plus what I needed for my taxi home.

At the bar now, they consider me an expert on fat girls. A luminary. I have told my story to many a tourist, how a succulent fat girl rescued me from a sexual jam. They respect me. In here. But out there as well. People point at me. The devil sucked off your wife, güey. But I don't care.

My little wife and I are intimate again. And whenever we finish making love, I caress her burn scars and she purrs like a kitten under a birch tree.

NOTES FOR A NEW THEORY FOR MASTERING HAIR

THE COWGIRL BIBLE had huge tits, a greasy face, and a mess of hair. From preadolescence, she had suffered flare-ups of rebellious hair. She learned early that letting loose those tresses was only possible for gals who could afford certain products. From the time she was just twelve or thirteen years old, as she entered the bloom of puberty, she focused blindly on the wild vertical porcupine that had begun to grow between her legs.

The punkospine, which had transmuted from the armadillo, developed in an onrush, like a flood, and could only be compared to the beards flaunted during certain musical phases by two members of ZZ Top. It could also be equated with the historic materialism of a certain identifiable and renowned pubis. The Cowgirl Bible suffered. She suffered from the folklorish dimensions of that wild bush. Her pubisexy mop could not hide under a bikini. It didn't matter how many atonal rakes she employed to shave, or how many blades she ordered from the hair-removal industry's complete catalog of new products, the punkospine always overwhelmed the emergent hairs like shrapnel, as is so often the case with certain honky-tonk gals.

During countless encounters with her mane, she avoided trying to control its erratic growth, until the day she was discovered by a buoyant hair talent scout. Once she found a skilled manipulator for her estimable hair of the loins, The Cowgirl Bible became the most committed participant in the national contest *Shave Your Triangle*. She won various awards in the ingrown hair category. At fifteen, she won the contest's most important honors: The Golden Porcupine, the equivalent of the Hotsprings Award for the Radioactive Bud.

When a competitor is awarded the top prize, she should retire. Traditionally, Goodbye My Love plays at these affairs. And because pubic hair was her life, The Cowgirl Bible said that telenovelas and hosting would not be her path. A change of scene meant only one thing: to go under the knife, to invest in plastic surgery the way one does with horse racing. She decided it was better to follow the example of certain ex-baseball players who become minor league coaches upon retirement. She would impose herself in stylology, specializing in the pubis. She had memorized the exact manipulation of the mini mini electric shaver they used to shave her before every catwalk competition.

The Cowgirl Bible was a living legend. She had been inducted into the hall of fame at fifteen. She was the youngest ever to conquer the big screen. No one didn't know who she was in the Guorl circuit®. But that didn't keep her from signing up for the hair removers' union under the snooty alias Ms. Las Vegas. As was tradition with novices, her first razor was a used one. A red Yamaha with white frets.

The secret to being a virtuous master of the blade, according to the first lesson from her virtual instructor on *The World's Great Epilators* DVD, not only resides in worshiping the divine mandate of shaving, but also in never forgetting the fundamental principle: that the music is in the wires. Handling an acoustic razor is not the same as handling an electric one. Check out the style.

The style is the man (or, in this case, the gluttonous little girl, or whoever occurs to me). That's the trick, the plan, the gift. It might come from heaven or as a spark of ingenuity. Some people say the key is in the tube amp, others lift the strings with their hands as they arpeggio or use a homemade instrument.

From the Yamaha, she went on to a Fender Stratocaster, which she called Lucille. She dreamed of shaving next to the greats. On the wall above her bed she had a giant poster of her hero, her holy moly, her one and only: Jaimito Hendrics. As a pre-celebrity teen, she'd go out on the streets with her razor hanging off her back and get together with her buddies, all aspiring virtuosos, and they'd watch video clips featuring Hendrics, this dude who played the razor with his teeth, threw it against the speakers, and lit it on fire.

Already marked as a product of the ghetto, she made her first public appearance at Cabelo do Porco, the PopSTock! interracial fair. Before, as was the case with all the aspirants, she'd taken part in small jams at highway bars and in neighborhood garages. She'd even had a small trio called Confessions of a Fried-Chicken Peddler. The power trio, rock's analectic formation, was the gospel she needed to follow. As models there were two of the most reputable groups in history (now gone): Cream and The Experience.

The interracial show consisted of lining up prospects before they went up onstage, as if they were waiting at a bank. On the stage, a group—razor, bass, and drums—was improvising on the pubis of a top model. The novice had to better, or at least equal, the rock and roll rapture of the stationary shaver going at another bush. Whoever managed to advance to the next phase, to be decided by the auditorium crowd, would compete in the last round for a Marshall amp, a car, two thousand pesos cash, and a Sony Ericsson cellphone.

As if she was getting in line to cash a pension check, The Cowgirl Bible took her place in that long queue. Just before it was her turn, the girl in front of her warned her not to go onstage. She'd only make a fool of herself. But our girl didn't give a shit. Decided, The Cowgirl Bible climbed the backstage steps.

—What is your name? asked the house band's razor player.

—The Cowgirl Bible.

—Where have you played?

—Around.

—Ladies and gentlemen, The Cowgirl Bible, from around.

The competition started. First up was the local, then the visitor. The local organized her model's pubes into a tiny pair of angel wings. The bass and drums never stopped improvising. Then The Cowgirl Bible launched into her performance.

She started calmly, too sweet for rock and roll. But then the performance went out of control. The Cowgirl Bible was out of this world. She was operating on a whole other beat, which, because it was new, sounded out of tune and awkward. The bass and drums interrupted the song. The model feared for her parts. The audience was disconcerted. The Cowgirl Bible hadn't realized there was absolute silence in the room except for the hum of her instrument. Everybody was completely focused on her, and she was completely focused on playing. To make her come back, the drummer took a plate from a pile and threw it on the ground. The sound of it smashing on the floor brought The Cowgirl Bible out of her abstract pyrotechnics. The test was over. The audience started laughing and jeering, and The Cowgirl Bible came down from the platform sad and lonely, as if she'd just swallowed some matches.

The Cowgirl Bible first heard about Crossroad in a documentary. If, as I suspect, her biographer is Latino, then her story will be titled *Encrucijada*. Perhaps they'll also make a movie. It will star Karen Bach. The soundtrack will win a Grammy®. Then there'll be a tribute by some black blues players. A street in the Bronx will be named after her and, finally, they will erect a statue of her along a path in Central Park and the inscription will read: *The Cowgirl Bible Parker Iniesta Herbert Novo. The cursed poet of electric shavers.*

But I am getting ahead of myself, being too cute for words, and a little nasty. Before The Cowgirl Bible appeared on the covers of all the magazines, before she became the great mother hen, godmother to all the girls, mother of Marianne Faithfull, she suffered for a second time. She suffered from the futility of being a fledgling. And this is off the record: After her failure in the contest she thought about abandoning—definitively and without the option of Methadone, like a beautiful trauma—her love of the bush-sculpting art.

That night after the concert, when all the bars had closed like wounds, she discovered Crossroad on TV. The documentary showed a mephitic location in the midst of a mythic nothing. It featured two paths that came together to form a cross. Or an X. Depending. On one side there was a bar attended to by a blind man, where they only served cola. Out in front, on a humble veranda, a deaf black man pretended to play guitar on a stick. They say a few meters up ahead there used to be a boot store called El Infierno, but nothing in the registers indicates such a thing. There is absolutely nothing there now.

Everything I've told of so far is relevant to the story because legend has it that if you can't figure out the signs, you won't be able to make a deal in Crossroad. If there's just one missing scenic element, then the journey will be harrowing, like dealing with a bureaucrat. If, by a stroke of bad luck, the bar is closed or the black guy is just meowing, then it will be necessary to return during lobster season. If by virtue of the Holy Child Jesus of Peyote, patron of PopSTock!, the requirements are met, then the devil will present himself at Crossroad at midnight, and you can make a deal. In exchange for your soul, you can even ask for press credentials.

The documentary had testimony from people who asked for the wildest things. One guy was happy with a lifetime season ticket to see his favorite soccer team. Granted. Another wanted to play the drums in Beck's band. But Beck wouldn't change his Christian drummer, he was too good. Yet a soul is like a caress, it's never unwelcome. So, in order to not squander his wish, the devil granted him a job as a percussionist. The last case was that of Old Man Paulino, the prestigious composer of El Mono de Alambre (whoever can't dance to that can just go fuck themselves), who traded his soul for a pair of leather boots from The Cowboy Bible.

At the end of the documentary, there were various fine-print clauses. But there was only one warning to those who might dare introduce themselves to the devil. The warning was not to do it while drunk. Contrary to popular song, Satan can't stand drunks. Showing up intoxicated to meet him runs the risk of him putting you in charge of the municipal dog pound or making you a Green Party volunteer for some political cause.

If, as Santi Carrillo proposes, music journalism is just a bourgeois extravagance, then we can understand the reviews that followed The Cowgirl Bible's first presentation, what we might call a comeback, with her new trio: The Midnight Angel of Oil for Cars:

> *The lewdness The Cowgirl Bible Parker deploys so directly reflects the nearly endless pubis she's had available during almost the entire tour of England she's just completed. It's part of one of the rhythmic patterns that have become her trademark during that time. During the intro and the verse we can hear the drums, the blade, and the bass playing in unison through an upbeat 7/4. The emphatic gestures come before and after the beat in a way that's totally innovative for heavy metal, especially when the band emphasizes the bass-drum pattern. At other times, it's more conventional, as in the razor solo, which is nonetheless very effective. The Cowgirl Bible's solo is like a high spiritual scream and evolves to a sonorous seduction, intensified by the use of the Octavia and its shameless adornments. It's one of The Cowgirl Bible's most inventive interludes, complete with phrases that she builds on as if she were talking to herself.*

Portinarismos aside, and no longer the amateur who'd been invited to perform only at informal gatherings and cocktail parties, The Cowgirl Bible turned out to be a real virtuoso on the wah-wah pedal. As with Jesus's life, a part of The Cowgirl Bible's life runs perpendicular to this narrative, without our knowing her whereabouts. There's a hole in the story. If indeed INRI went into seclusion in the desert to talk with YHWH, in an anti-apocryphal version of Vicente Fernández's song, *Hoy platiqué con mi gallo*, The Cowgirl Bible Parker, on the B-side, also decided to seclude herself in the desert, according to certain non-canonical gospels, to make a deal with the State's unholy lover, Satan. This happened between her visit to Crossroad and her triumphant comeback. It was about a three-year period. What was The Cowgirl Bible's address during this time? Could it be true she was abducted by Egyptian extraterrestrial telenovela addicts? Was this foretold in Jaime Pausán's prophecies? Remain in your seats. After the talk we'll open up for questions.

Jesus fled to the desert so he wouldn't be seduced by evil's gourmet desserts: flan, egg custard, rice pudding, pastries, cookies, *sodacerveza sodacerveza*, *gorditas*, *chicharrón picadillo gorditas* in mole, *lonches lonches lonches*, and masks masks masks bring your masks we've got a Místico el Huracán Ramírez Damián 666 mask, send your boy send your gal we'll give you three packs of caguama for six caramel apples, tamales tamales we have hot tamales, yes you heard right for just forty pesos we're gonna let you have two pairs of socks four swim suits and a shawl today only and before eight p.m. c'mon up close, for your mother-in-law the plague spider fly cockroach bring your roach powder bring it bring it, a watermelon fat watermelon Chinese watermelon sweet five for ten pesos, red melon red melon red, a little something for the love of God ma'am I'm just trying to get enough for fare to Juárez I'm gonna cross the border to join up with my *carnal* who's in Elay I'll sweep your street wash your car mow your lawn in the name of the little virgin of Guadalupop even if it's just a taco ma'am may God repay you with many children and may God keep you in his Holy Glory amen, etc.

The Cowgirl Bible didn't have to go anywhere. She was already in the desert. So she went to meet the Boss of Bosses. Respected at every level. Old and wise: Satan.

This is how it happened:

But first, a problem that all systole narratives face: how to represent the devil. Is it true or false that he appears as a mantelpiece, or as the folkloric figure in the Mexican lottery? *Chalupa y buenas.* To try and solve the problem, we can humangenomemap it in three ways:

A Appealing to the common denominator. That is, like Ned Flanders;
B Like a *culiche* boxer before he steps into the ring. With Los Huracanes del Norte's song, Lincoln negro, like an idiosyncratic headline;
C Refuting the theory that God is black, and sponsoring evil as such from November 2nd, 19**. A chocolate devil.

This would explain a whole shitload of stuff. First, that the dubbing of this equation would be double-spaced, that the devil would be well endowed, and, lastly, that The Cowgirl Bible would adopt blues and soul roots as her musical model, without giving up the best licks and tricks used by white blues and psychedelic axers. Satan told her: Jaimito Hendrics always played black material. With the following exceptions: Cream, a little Dylan, The Beatles, and The Troggs' Wild Thing.

The Cowgirl Bible's success, like gears on a car, rested on four foundational perspectives. First, second, third, and fourth: the historic appearances she made at the London bar Bag O'Nails before the stars of British razordom.*

That's why, when The Cowgirl Bible returned to her homeland, PopSTock! of the drunken crazies, the audience got used to the syntax of her instrument as easily as an IMSS nurse learns to ignore patients. That's how intoxicating The Cowgirl Bible's sound became for the neo-public. Neglected compatriots who come to in the sanatorium, here's your meal your bed your nurse, who hit you buddy. Rock it. Especially if it's your first record. *The polar bear robs robs robs me*, gets a rating of ten from the untamable critics. The next step is to get billed as the warm-up act on a Coca-Cola sponsored tour. And from there it's gravy.

That is, until the day the following warning popped up on The Cowgirl Bible's computer:

BRONTOK.A [10]

—Hentikan kebobrokan di negeri ini —

1. Penjarakan Koruptor, Penyelundup, Tukang Suap & Bandar NARKOBA

(Send to NUSAKAMBANGAN)

* Kevin Ayers, who was in the audience, remembers with certain incredulity: All the stars were there and I heard all the important terms, like, you know, shit, Jesus, damn, and other, worse words.

2. Stop Free Sex, Aborsi & Prostitusi
(Go To HELL)
3. Stop pencemaran lingkungan, pembakaran hutan & perburuan liar
4. SAY NO TO DRUGS!!!
— KIAMAT SUDAH DEKAT —
Terinspirasi oleh:
Elang Brontok (Spizaetus Cirrhatus) yang hampir punah
[By HVM3l]
—JowoBot #VM Community —
!!! Akan Kubuat Mereka (VM lokal yg cengeng & bodoh) Terkapar!!!

OMG. Is that hot enough? The previous warning doesn't mean what it means. Anita, sit next to Billy ain't the same as sit on the billy. In fact, the warning said the devil needed The Cowgirl Bible's soul. It was time. To pay up. If you should see that warning on your screen, be very very careful, it's a sign you're pretty much done for. It'd be best to seek refuge, just in case the Hacienda, Quinta, and Rancho all come down on you.

Hey, Devil, no worries, I'm gonna pay up, just hold the carnitas, let me keep the tamales. That's what The Cowgirl Bible wanted to say, but she didn't get a chance. The evil one had arrived. And time, dear spectator, time is pop. The Devil is pop. Love is pop. And pop is a whore. From that moment on, The Cowgirl Bible had no choice but to avoid at all costs the disgraceful signs of pop. Like, for example, playing the lottery. And since she was a wrestling addict, she avoided all matches that featured the Evil team, such as Satánico or the DEA's Arcángel. She fed her paranoia to such an extent that she stopped consuming *vampiros*, with their salsa verde, refrain of refried beans, hot tortillas, and icy Victoria beers. How she'd loved them. Too bad. But no tears.

Before any more of this blah blah blah, prepared by Lexus and based on a plan boosted by HarperCollins, we're gonna pay attention to the regression hypnosis that will reveal, via The Cowgirl Bible's own words, the strategy that should be used by anyone interested in selling their soul to the Devil:

> The crossroads are at El Cerro de la Cruz. Famous for its *cholos* and male prostitutes and, oh, for the quality of the coke sold there. Don Devil himself begins the auditions after midnight and a toke. According to some folks, he could start earlier but he never misses the five o'clock telenovela and at around eight he takes off for the gym. He dines

at ten and then, yeah, the proceedings begin. I'd been told the lines could get as long as a bank's, or like those at soccer stadium box offices. But I was pretty much by my lonesome. Maybe because it was Sunday and everybody was still hungover. There were just four of us. There was a man in front and, oh, how he loved to argue. It was Old Man Paulino, a *corridos* composer determined to show Satan that spiders are oviparous. I'd also been told Don Chamuco liked a little pussy. But it wasn't true. The truth is that when it was my turn, he treated me with cool efficiency. I was told to go to window number four for a stamp, then to number twelve for various signatures, and then at the register I finally signed the contract for one soul. I waited fifteen days for my new aptitudes to arrive via DHL.

When I count to three and clap my hands, The Cowgirl Bible will wake up and not remember any of this. So, one two three, and you're back, said the very portrait of the salon's teenage cowboybiblish hypnotist. Now, let's dismiss the doctor. Thank you for your help. Please pick up your honorarium. Thank you.

And now let's return to the story.

The words quoted above, directly from The Cowgirl Bible, are excerpted from the book *Black Magic: Real or Mental Cumbia?*, authored by Dr. RHA. During various periods, more or less from cool to post-cool, The Cowgirl Bible thought that by going to therapy she could rid herself of her belief in Satan, and that way she'd be free of her deal and it'd be impossible to take her soul. But no way, you can't play crooked on the king of crooks, lord and master of smuggling, software piracy, and made-in-China Virgins of Guadalupe. Time takes its toll, and it wasn't long (a space of about five centimeters that's found between the fingers when spread out as if the hand were a kite) before The Cowgirl Bible felt the twenty-three grams of her soul being seized.

It was a year, then two, that the Devil hadn't shown his face at PopSTock!. He was very busy, with Jorge Reinoso, representing malice in Almada films. Around that time, The Cowgirl Bible's third record debuted at the peak of the Top 40 lists, right at number one. Her single, Subscribe to Marie Claire, was nominated for song of the year by Esténcil Miusic Aguords because of its use of pastiche, le collage, and cats-up with the electric razor.

And then it happened: She was invited to take part in the recording of Celso Piña's DVD, *Cumbia Power*. Celebrating his twenty-five years of playing *vallenato*, the DVD would capture a live concert of Celso's hits accompanied by various invited guests. This was, both superficially and at the deepest level, a helluva privilege: to play alongside PopSTock!'s favorite son. Only a very select group of artists would play with Celso onstage, which seemed to indicate that The Cowgirl Bible's career had been forged by fire and would come roaring out of the flames. Could she—drunk and drugged—dance naked to The Return of the Son of Monster Magnet* and keep her rep unscathed? She, had, in fact, already done it at some party. In time, that would become one of The Cowgirl Bible's very few appearances on film.

The Cowgirl Bible could barely remember Hungry Daddy Freaky Satan when, out of the blue, another messenger appeared to muddy the waters. Be careful, warrior girl, because the feds are looking for you, they warned

* Unfinished Ballet in Two Tableau: 1. Ritual Dance of Child-Killer. Il Nullis Petti (*no* commercial potential) is what freaks sound like when you turn them loose in a recording studio at one o'clock in the morning with five hundred dollars' worth of rented percussion equipment. A bright snappy number. Hotcha!

her. At a personal level, this kind of threat can be used to rationalize a farewell tour, featuring the corresponding DVD and the enjoyment of many accompanying honors. How many celebrities, late in life, at the time of their death, would take care of their business on Earth so that they could leave in peace? Not a one. The Cowgirl Bible didn't either, so she didn't worry about inquiring, or arranging with her label for the remastering of her work, or leaving as a final request that she be cremated and that her ashes be scattered in the desert by the Estación Marte. She spent her time just sanfernanding, that is, spending some time on her feet, then doing some pacing, all in wait of the biggest villain in *el cine de ficheras*: the devil.

The omens played out exactly like the saying The pig with the thickest lips will get the best ear of corn. First, there was a scarcity of pot in the state. It was a tragedy of Dostoyevskian proportions because, with their soothing weed gone, the potheads had turned into dangerous creatures of unclassifiable sorts. They were stuck seeking work as mini-golf caddies, pizza-delivery persons, fried-chicken peddlers. Second, the local team fell into a ten-game losing streak. The city was a neurotic chaos, and in each home we saw unchained scenes of unnecessary violence. Third, the idiots working for the city forgot to spray for dengue and the mosquitos went on an epidemiological spree.

As the omens got more intense, the devil's presence seemed more palpable. But still Satan didn't appear. And he won't appear, somebody said. For these kind of gigs, he counted on proxies, gangster lawyers, licensed trinketeers, magicians, flatterers, politicians, conspirators, scribners, tramps, black-market runners, umpires, arbiters, referees, beatniks, pencil pushers, tunicked eunuchs, hippies, etc. As soon as the soul was taken, the devil entrusted the act to a minion. He hated his clients, he bitched that they were all whiners, always asking for postponements. Just like concertgoers, they wanted more, an encore, one more, one more, one more. The Cowgirl Bible just didn't know. She didn't realize the agent she'd hired to contract her for a show on the El Paso highway was actually at the service of the Axis of Evil International Company. She had accepted. I've had it up to here with hiding from this cabrón, she said. He's supposed to be the hottest tamale in the world, but he always winds up mocked in Hollywood-style rom-coms. A little show on the border with minimum backup is gonna help me get over so much delirium.

*

She arrived in Juárez on a Transportes del Norte bus. She watched two movies on the trip. *The Devil Wears Prada* and *The Day of the Beast*. From Juárez she hopped over to El Paso. Texas smelled insufferably of plagiarism. When the air smells so strongly of imitation, it can only mean one thing: sulfur. The gossipy sulfur that indicates the devil* is once more among the people.

The Cowgirl Bible knew that establishing herself in the USA was a task for talking machines. Satan's powers were like those of Corona beer: It was unfazed by borders. Or perhaps as potent as the services offered by UPS (which was suddenly shit too). Evil depends on express delivery. So as not to continue her avoidance, The Cowgirl Bible didn't move; whatever happened, she would confront her rival. The power of the highest high is the power of the highest high. Here, there, over here or over there, or a little more over here, right here, right right here; there you go, right there. There it was. A perfect place for an altar.

*

---

* Please note that the Devil is sometimes in lower case and other times in upper case. The reason is that sometimes there isn't enough respect to hit the upper case (a tardy infomercial from the intratranslator).

At midnight, she entered the bar with the epic all-encompassing patience of an à la carte menu before it's even been read. But there was no sign of the devil, not even his gleaming sandals. He was flying the colors of the Mexican All-Stars at a game against Panama in Houston. In his place, and to go on with the show, the devil had sent his top doggest of top dogdom: Steve Vai, who, in less time than it takes to fill a fried-chicken order, challenged The Cowgirl Bible to a razor duel. She knew she couldn't turn it down. To refuse a dignified death meant, in times of Reformation, to spend all of eternity wandering the Juárez market bathrooms.

For the contest, they brought in two of the hairiest pubises in all of history: those of Tongolele and María Victoria (the one who sings really slowly... really, really slowly). The solos began. For eight minutes of strenuous improvisation, not a hair was seen on the blades. It was only when the music began to play, indicating that the participants had gone over time and it was time to go to commercial, that the competitors stopped. The jury's decision was this:

> The Cowgirl Bible's performance is well structured, and keeps an adequate razor beat as it subscribes

> to an innovative meta-language. It's a modern approach, and without skimping on its virtues, bold.
>
> When shaving, Steve Vai connected with a stale tradition and was able to liven it up. The rich razor mix keeps his score up. There's no need to divorce the anethaeum of the *carpa*.

And that, my dear friends, was the last time anyone laid eyes on The Cowgirl Bible Parker. That was just a few minutes ago, since the final duel with Steve Vai was recorded on a cellphone and uploaded to YouTube. We don't know what happened next. The video cuts off. There's a crazy theory that it was all a setup, that The Cowgirl Bible isn't dead. That she faked her own death because she'd had it up to here with so much fame. Some loyal fans swear they've seen her buying fried chicken at several Henry's franchises. Others are sure she's living in India and using an English colonizer name. It doesn't matter. We have The Cowgirl Bible on YouTube, to watch as often as we desire.

In a little while, when the battle against global warming is lost, it will only be possible to watch the real Cowgirl

Bible on YouTube. The devil will only be invoked through the worldwide web. If you want to keep her life from ending, just send a donation to 1-800-YouTube. With your contribution, we can guarantee that, even if it's just on a screen, the real Cowgirl Bible will go on and on thanks to the internet.

For more information, search for the guitar duel with Steve Vai on YouTube.

NEITHER FICTION NOR NON-FICTION

THE POST-NORTEÑO CONDITION

I was born norteño to the extreme.

CUCO SÁNCHEZ

1

And:

—My boots.

—Huh?

—Have you seen my lice-skin boots, my dear? You remember that pair, right?

—Yes.

—Yes, what?

—Oh, Paulino, you've lost it. Those were Cowboy Bible boots. You've never had lice-skin boots.

—Those very ones. Find them for me. I wanna strap 'em on.

—You wore them out. Don't you remember? You wouldn't take them off, not even to climb the mezquite tree.

—It's just that those were real boots and not these thankless stilts that make each step such a misfortune.

—Take them off. They're just a burden. Let your feet air out.

—Later. How else am I gonna walk out of here?

—Put on some other ones.

—Which ones?

—You're like a woman. You have a closet full of boxes of boots but you can't make up your mind. Don't you have a pair that'll go with your pants?

—Well, it's just that all those mules are just as lame as these.

—Try some new ones. Open up a box and even if they're a little rough at first, you can break them in.

—No, it's better if I just buy a new pair.

—Oh no, Paulino. More boots? There's no room for more in the closet. Where am I gonna put my shoes and dresses?

—Don't you worry, my love. We'll make sure there's a secret drawer so you can stow away all your footwear and costumes. We'll make it just like on those pot-smuggling trucks.

2

In the meantime, Old Man Paulino, free of his lady's demands, showed up all tired and tanned at the small Botas Roca shop. Since the Old Man was a distinguished citizen of San Pedrosburgo, he was attended to by a clerk who was a walking encyclopedia on norteño style boots.

—Don Paulino, what brings you here?

—Oh, why are you so simple? I came to get some boots, dummy.

—I just received a shipment of contraband. All new, Don Paulino, all new.

—Bring them all out. I wanna see them all, even the exotic ones.

—Look how beautiful this is: blue-whale loin, and certified authentic. Let me know what caliber you want. Or these, just look at this authentic *Nosferatu* zeal. Try them on. I also have some Komodo dragon ones. See how gorgeous they are.

—You're silly, boy. Those look like wrestler boots.

—I'm gonna show you the river dolphin ones.

—Stop, stop. I'm looking for a pair of Cowboy Bible boots.

—Oh, Don Paulino. You've lost it, you're off-key. They don't make those anymore. They're off the market because they hurt the ozone layer.

3

—I told you, Paulino. But you just keep forgetting. There are no Cowboy Bible-skin boots left in this world.

—You're so right, my love. These two stones were meant for the same bird: I could neither get the boots I wanted nor find any that would bring me comfort.

—Paulino, don't be so stoic. Use any of the boots in the closet. That's what they're there for.

—No, my love. Those shall remain unworn.

—Then why did you buy them?

—Oh, my dear wife. The value of certain boots is precisely in keeping them intact, just like that. As soon as I put them on, I would take away all their charm.

—Hey, Paulino, if they don't make those boots in factories anymore, what about having them handmade?

—That's exactly what I was asking about, a homemade version. The problem is the leather. It's very scarce. They say The Cowboy Bible is in danger of extinction.

—What if you ordered them from McAllen?

—They don't have it in Texas either. It's a very tough leather. I'm fucked.

—Don't cry. Just give up, Paulino.

—Give up? Not me. I'm a meaner cabrón than I am good-looking. I'm gonna get my Cowboy Bible boots even if I have to sell my soul to the devil.

—Oh Paulino. You've lost it. Again? How many times have you sold your soul to the devil?

—I know. But it doesn't count drunk. This time I'm gonna make the offer sober. Those other times don't count, they don't.

4

Such coveted boots, they finally showed up. But on somebody's else's feet.

It was spread all over San Pedro, the federal capital, by word of mouth. It's rumored a foreign man was seen wearing boots that, if not Cowboy Bible boots, sure looked like them.

It was only then that Old Man Paulino, ready to deal, stepped unsteadily up to the guy and told him the boots had inspired a corrido.

—Indulge me, buddy, and tell me something. The leather on those boots—is it original Cowboy Bible?

—Yeah, they're no fakes.

—*Original* original?

—ISO quality.

—Where'd you pick them up?

—El Infierno.

—Where?

—El Infierno shoe store.

—What size are those?

—Seven and three eighths.

—Look, I'm a seven and then some. Let me ride 'em?

—What the hell, Don Paulino. Absolutely.

—Oh my.

—What, Don Paulino?

—I'm stuck, I can't get them on. What screw did you tighten, boy? They just need to be a pinch bigger to fit me to a T.

—I see. They're just not new new. They've molded to my feet.

—That can be undone. A little swim and they'll sweeten to mine.

—Ah, Don Paulino. You've lost it. You know Cowboy

Bible boots: If they're not custom-made, they'll crack. They only do what they're made to do. They don't get tempted by other feet, even the sun's.

5

—My love.

—Yes, Paulino.

—I'm going on a trip.

—So soon? Oh, Paulino. Don't drive yourself mad with this.

—My love, my affinity for those boots cannot be ignored.

—Did you have lunch already?

—No.

—I'll make you some of your favorite tacos for the road.

—I don't have time for that. My horses and men are waiting to devote themselves to the task.

—Oh, Paulino. You've lost it. It's bad not to have even one bean dancing in those two kilometers of intestine when you go shopping.

—Oh my love, those are women's concerns. I'm just going out for a pair of boots.

—Get a grip, Paulino. There are risks. They've said cold

front number eight is headed this way. You have to bear that in mind.

—Don't make assumptions, my love. People who are supposed to be so smart about the weather always make false prophecies. They're like those boastful bettors. They always pick the wrong cock.

—Let's hope so. Let's hope you don't catch a chill and get sick from all that cold.

—Don't even say it, my love. I won't lose it. I'll present myself completely whole and uninjured. Just remember that with a kilo of tequila, a double poncho, and sarape, you can scare away any chill.

6

—I'm not lying Don Paulino. You've lost it. I've already explained that according to everything the foreigner said, El Infierno shoe store should be right here.

—You sure?

—Absolutely. This is where the store should be.

—We have to investigate.

—We've already looked and looked all over the place. It's not there.

—Are you sure those are the right coordinates?

—Yes, boss. Look: To be sure, there's the crossroad, the railroad tracks, and the little joint where they sell cured meat. El Infierno should be right across there.

—And what did the bartender say?

—That there's no latitude for what we're looking for. That he's already told the herd. That a wasteland isn't the place for a shoe store. That El Infierno was never here. Not even temporarily.

—Maybe we're too scattered? Maybe it's over the hill?

—No, Don Paulino. We're in the right place. There's the black guy. Remember what the foreigner said. At the crossroad, where you see the black guy playing guitar on a stick, that's where El Infierno should be.

7

—You've lost it, Paulino. From all that trotting. I saw you from a distance and knew it was you.

—We never found the shoe store, my love.

—And how did you expect to find it if you didn't take anything with you? You left without a scapular, without lunch or a map.

—We had a compass. But it broke at the crossroad. It couldn't be coaxed to signal south at south or north at north.

—Oh Paulino, I've told you, to orient yourself use the sun's rays, the position of the stars, or the wind's caress on a finger swathed in spit.

8

—I've done everything in this life: collected horses, boots, and fine roosters. But I've never been a quitter.

—Enough, Paulino. Forget about the boots.

—No, my love. I can't give up.

—Oh Paulino. Come on. You've lost it. What about when you promised to compose a corrido for the rustler they ambushed in Buenos Aires, Coahuila?

—I was using my head. Anyway, I'm in a better place to inspire songs than to come up with one.

—Stop, Paulino. They've discontinued Cowboy Bible boots. They took them off the market because you were the only one buying them.

—I'll disappear before that happens, my love.

—Believe me.

—No. I've decided. I have to sell my soul to the devil.

—You, you're crazy.

—I'm gonna sell my soul to the devil. I'm gonna sell it like they sell trucks: whole or in parts.

—Are you serious, Paulino?

—Yes, my love.

—And you believe that?

—Believe what?

—That Satan is gonna come running like Chabelo to offer you a gift in exchange for your soul?

—Why not? Everybody has their thing. There's Cojo Martínez's *valseada*, who spent twenty years in a wheelchair and, after just one little chat with the devil, was busy showing off the two dancing legs she got for her engagement ring.

—Oh Paulino. You've lost it. You've got brain freeze. That's material for corridos. That only happens in corridos. Paulino, corridos are not the same as real life.

9

—For two nights, I stood and screamed and screamed but the devil didn't show.

—By yourself, Don Paulino?

—By my lonesome. And I went through four packs of cigarettes.

—And tequila?

—Two kilos of help. It's goddamn chilly trying to conjure up the devil out there in the open. Actually, pour me another. A double. What do you mean which one, dummy—the same one Pedro Infante drinks! Tradicional.

—Ah, I see, Don Paulino. You've completely lost it. Everybody knows the devil sidles up a street in Cerro de la Cruz at midnight. You just make yourself known and, if there's a line, don't get in it. You present your credentials—Old Man Palvino, corridos composer—and state your case.

—Imagine. And here I've been warming up.

—Is it true you're gonna sell your soul to the devil?

—Of course not, dummy. If I did, then where would my corridos come from?

—So what are you gonna offer him?

—A pedicure for his rooster foot and a horseshoe for his goat's foot.

—Ah, sure, Don Paulino, always kidding around.

—Don't doubt me, güey. I'm gonna make him swallow something that's not gonna come back up. My sorrel horse.

The most beautiful of all my mares. His eyes are gonna pop out. He's gonna accept the deal. He's gonna accept because no one—not even the devil—has ever had such a beautiful mare.

10

—Who goes there?

—Me.

—Ah, you. Don Paulino. How are you?

—As good as when I killed the deceased.

—So you're over your drunkenness?

—Come now, it's not like it's contagious.

—What brings you around these parts?

—I've come to sell you my soul.

—No, no, no, not in your condition. You're wasted.

—Well, I've been partying, buddy.

—Yes, I see, but I don't make deals like that. Wait till it passes and when you've got your senses, then come back.

—No, just this once. While I'm stoked. Whatever's gonna happen, let it happen. Why make me come and go senselessly?

—Paulino, you don't understand, you've lost it. How many times have you offered me your soul? And each time, you're drunk as a skunk. Go home. Sleep it off, like you always do. Come back sober. You know I won't bargain otherwise. No deal.

—What a fag of a devil you are. Just once. I won't regret it. Don't they always say kids and drunks always tell the truth. Goddamn grouchy old man.

11

—Next.

—Good evening.

—Ah, it's you, Paulino. How are you doing?

—Fresh. Sober. Bathed.

—Now then. What's your business?

—I've come to sell you a mare at a loss for a pair of Cowboy Bible boots.

—Not interested. Next.

—She's a breed. Pure blood. Look how haughty she is.

—Yes, I see she's a blueblood, but I'm not good with animals or plants. It's just gonna die on me.

—Then I offer you my soul.

—It doesn't interest me either.

—Then my song royalties.

—I'm immune to norteño music. I don't like corridos or norteño music.

—I've got nothing else. I have nothing else with which to entice you.

—Yes, you do: your wife.

—You're out of your mind, man. If my wife finds out I'm trafficking with her soul, she'd kill me.

—I'm not interested in her soul. I just wanna sleep with her one time.

—You're hopeless, man. You're twisted. She'd never accept. And she'd murder me first.

—Insist. Insist until you convince her.

—Don't count on it. If I even mention it, the least that will happen is that she'll have me diagnosed as senile and put me in diapers and never let me out of her sight for the rest of our lives.

12 THE KID'S ALL TWISTED

A play in one act

Characters: The devil and Old Man Paulino

A country road, a tree. Dusk. Paulino, sitting on the ground, is filling a tank. He's exhausted and making a big effort, using both hands. He pauses, so tired, rests, pants, sighs. Repeats same gestures.

Enter The Devil (the audience applauds).

THE DEVIL: Hey. Considering you're someone so used to liquor and pot, you should be okay, Paulino. How are you doing?

PAULINO: Better, don't you think?

THE DEVIL: You look tired, *mi estilos*. What's wrong, Old Man?

PAULINO: My wife.

THE DEVIL: Oh, Paulino. You've totally lost it. With those legs, your wife could make any man ache.

PAULINO: Even you. Satan himself. The least clandestine of all massage-parlor clients.

THE DEVIL: Even me.

PAULINO: Shall we smoke a little weed?

THE DEVIL: Later. To get some balance. But the weed aside, what's bothering you, dude?

PAULINO: My wife is being subversive. On top of not wanting to take a tumble with you, she informed me she wants to go to the Valentín Elizalde dance. I'm not gonna take her. It makes me wanna sneak her some *yombina*, to see if she gets hot enough so I can get my boots.

THE DEVIL: I'll give you an easier recipe. Let's put on a farce: We'll go to your house and pretend to have a poker bet. You bet your money and lose. All your assets, you lose them. In the end, you bet a roll in the hay with your wife and you lose.

PAULINO: I don't think she'll go for it. She's not a big fan of card games.

THE DEVIL: You let her know I'm taking everything. That if she consents, I'll reconsider the debt. If she accepts I won't toss you out on the street.

13

—Where'd it happen?

—In Mole's bar.

—Oh Paulino, if you're always losing it, why'd you bet?

—Then what, my love?

—No, Paulino. I'm not some song lyric. You're not gonna use me as currency with some card shark.

—But if you don't agree, we'll never have another meal at El Rey del Cabrito. It's not even one night, my love. He's a good person.

—Doesn't matter how decent. You think I'm in condition to be traded like peanuts?

—Well, the debt would be covered that way. He'd even owe me something.

—Paulino, tell me the truth. How much did you lose?

—Everything.

—Even the Nativity?

—Yes, even those plaster figurines.

—They're porcelain.

—Whatever. Assholes, those damn figurines.

—You're sick, Paulino. I refuse to sleep with a stranger just to fix your mess. I'm outta here. I'm going to my mother's. I wanna divorce.

—And what will you get out of that? I don't have a thing. Not the ranch or the rights to my songs, not even my gray hairs. But if instead you calm down and throw down with that card shark for a few, then it's like nothing ever happened.

—Paulino, tell me the truth. How much did you lose?

—Everything. Even the dirt under my nails.

—Well. Fine. I'll let you twist my arm. But to be clear I'm doing it only to keep us out of the poorhouse. Things are gonna change in this house. And you tell that man there's no guarantee I'm gonna give him my body. Make it very clear all I'll accept is an invitation to Valentín Elizalde's dance. Then we'll see.

14

—Don't come to me now with sob stories out of Vicente Fernández movies, Paulino. Gambling debts are matters of honor. Don't act like a fool.

—I've kept my end of the deal. The rest is up to you, pendejo.

—Don't be a fool.

—I did my part. She'll go with you to the dance. It's up to you to get her in bed.

—I said no, Paulino. Until your wife comes to me you're not gonna wear Cowboy Bible boots. Those were the terms.

—The only term and condition I value is that of the north. The norteño condition. The way all the guys who get tangled in these agreements refuse to furrow their brows. Damn devil, that's why I liked you.

—Oh, Paulino. You've lost it. Over and over. Wait a while and you'll have your boots at dawn. And I'll bring your woman back to you all happy happy. Content. Well taken care of.

—Listen, pendejo. You might be the devil, but you can just fuck off. No boots, no deal. And if you tell me one more time that I've lost it, I'm gonna kick your ass.

15

—Don't exaggerate, my love.

—But it's true, Paulino, you even owed your ass to that card shark.

—Not really.

—A saint must have intervened.

—Don't blaspheme, my love. When it comes to gambling, this comes with the territory.

—Oh Paulino, you've lost it. He took even the shirt off your back and left us homeless, propertyless, and corridoless. And then, suddenly, without an argument, he takes off. He left without so much as a raincheck. That had to have been because of a saint's intervention.

—Cross yourself, my love. Cross yourself. What's

important is that you no longer have to give that card shark anything. Not him or anyone else.

—Paulino.

—Huh?

—So I'm not going to the Valentín Elizalde dance anymore?

—Well, no.

—Paulino.

—Huh?

—Take me.

—No, no way. What the hell would I do at that faggot's dance anyway?

—Oh Paulino. Then give me permission to go.

—No.

—Listen, I'm not going alone. My sister will chaperon. C'mon. Why not. Nothing's gonna happen.

—How do you know, my love? No. I forbid you from going to the dance. I fear for you. The devil could be anywhere.

16

—The Grand Marquis.

—Which?

—The Grand Marquis.

—No, let's go in the truck.

—Why.

—He'll get suspicious. When he doesn't see the gray car, he'll know we're headed for the dance. Better a cab.

—Oh, sister, you're getting like Paulino. You're losing it. If you don't smoke, you don't imagine things. If we take a cab, then we're admitting to the crime.

—So then we walk?

—What? You're crazy.

—It's at the Terraza Riviera. It's close by.

—No. We're going in the Marquis, and we're gonna floor it.

—I'm afraid. If your husband catches us, he's gonna make mincemeat out of us. I can't take the thought of going to the hospital. Not even with the money I left in Houston.

—Don't be so dramatic. He's never gonna find out. And I don't think he'll be that mad even if he does.

—And what if something happens?

—What could possibly happen? Who's even gonna notice two little cowgirls in that multitude?

17

—Forgive me, Paulino.

—Don't get upset, my love.

—The doctor said I didn't have to stay in the hospital even one day. These are second-degree burns. I can heal at home.

—Don't get yourself all worked up. Rest.

—Paulino. Forgive me.

—I forgive you. But rest, rest. Don't get worked up, my love.

—How could I know that man with the hat from the dance had a tail of fire?

—What did he look like?

—Normal. Wore boots and a piteado belt with a twenty-centimeter buckle.

—What was his name?

—I don't know. He didn't tell me his name. He just approached me and asked me to dance. By the second song, my body was burning wherever he squeezed me.

—But you went on. Why didn't you call for help?

—I did. I screamed at the top of my lungs. That was after I saw his feet. They weren't human. He had a goat's hoof and a rooster's foot.

—Holy shit.

—Men in hats pulled their guns and shot at him. But nobody saw where he went. The devil showed up just to roast me and disappear.

—It's okay, my love. It's over.

—Paulino.

—Huh?

—Now you can write me a corrido. I was in all the newspapers. *Antes muerta que sencilla*: The Devil Invited Her to Dance.

—I'll write it for you, my love.

—Paulino.

—Huh?

—A while ago there was a nurse who came through here wearing boots like the ones you're looking for.

—Oh yeah. I saw them in a store window on my way to the hospital.

—They're selling them again?

—Yeah. The store clerk told me they were making them again.

—So why didn't you buy a pair? You wanted them so much.

—I lost it, my love. You already knew I lost it.

JUAN SALAZAR'S DEALER

For Pedro Rodríguez, El Viejo Cuervo

—DEALERS ARE ONLY GOOD for only one thing: breaking your heart.

—Into a thousand pieces.

—Oh, and composing corridos.

Juan Salazar, the most outstanding exponent of the narcocorrido, watched the lights of the New York subway with tenderness. The wee hours had left a string of bad luck in Times Square. They scurried past like scorpions, sparkling with rats and homeless paranoids. Notwithstanding the norteño singer's aplomb (signified by his Chesterfield coat, hat, and boots), the junkies would scrape together any little thing they could off the street for the love of smack. Heroin is always a tough love.

—Damn him. He seemed trustworthy.

—I warned you, Juan, said Herbert Huncke. That little dealer was all talk.

With the tenacity that the gold bracelet and Terlenka outfit allowed him, a languid Juan Salazar shoved his partner aside, staying faithful to the whim of the tracks. Without a glance at the drag queens, sotol still in hand (just in case), he felt a blue centrifugal lash at the back of his knees: It was withdrawal. But he didn't give up waiting for the dealer who would never come; he just remained indifferent, like a dove in the meadow.

—He's not coming, Juan. The dealer's not coming.

The performer of Cuatro Lágrimas felt his belt ease out of the loops on his jeans and slither like a snake in the sand. He wasn't afraid. He already knew that all the bullfights and cockfights taking place in the station were products of his withdrawal. The addict's own sweat would slow the passenger cars, and he would mentally transport himself to all those crazy, intrepid comings and goings with his arm around The Cowboy Bible, looking for the complete dealer.

His regression was contaminated by theories from bar stories about San Pedroslavia. A magical land. Endless drugs. Everyone a dealer. Super cheap heroin. Dissolute and feverish, Juan Salazar would keep his promise to move to Mexico. To settle in San Pedroslavia and benefit from the open heroin traffic.

—The dealer's not coming, Juan. We can still make the exchange at the pharmacy. Let's go before it gets dark.

Huncke was also going through his own struggle with cold turkey. He said withdrawal was like chewing a flavorless gum. The junky's waning quarter would soon become a full moon, and the station would fill with Aztec vampires just for him. But Juan Salazar remained unmoved, even after he understood how the exchange with the fraudulent pharmaceuticals worked. The only way to unload that Star .380 was to trade it to a dealer for thirty-five doses of heroin.

He'd been trying to unarm himself for a year. He'd drunk countless beers in his attempts to get rid of the pistol. No one would take it. The gun had acquired a rep as a bad omen. He went everywhere with the Star .380, and in the process became known for carrying it in a shoebox under his arm. He couldn't *give* it away, not even at a pawnshop.

—Juan, for the tenth time. The dealer blew you off. He's not coming.

—Juan, for the sicketh dulleth time. The dealer's a blow off. He's not coming, not coming, not coming... The phrases echoed in his head like the sound of the alto sax with his norteño group.

—It's impossible to get rid of this thing, isn't it?

—And to think you traded a typewriter for it.

Juan Salazar Pro, realizing that getting rid of the pistol was impossible in New York, decided to head to Mexico. Perhaps in San Pedroslavia it would not be so difficult to unload the gun. After all, what difference did it make if San Pedroslavia didn't turn out to be the paradise he imagined and was instead just another ruse? I can always come back to nourish my post-norteño condition on the streets of Manhattan, he thought.

—Huncke, let's go.

—And the dealer, Juan?

—I'm going to Mexico. To San Pedroslavia.

—And the dealer? We're not waiting for him anymore, Juan.

—Huncke. Let's go. Let's get out of here. Let's get out of here, because that dealer's not coming.

THE DEFINITIVE DEALER

Written on a wall in an unorthodox script with El Oso shoe polish was, The only way to get drugs is to *be* the drug. Pedro Rodríguez, an expert on norteño music, was sleeping in his attic room on Coahuila Street. An occasional session musician who imitated Chet Baker's norteño-ness, he had begun to shoot up heroin. His musical instrument was The Cowboy Bible.

The phrase on the wall had been pirated from a little book of poems by Jack Kerouac, Heroin is for Pain. There was a Juan Salazar LP on the record player. With that voice that always seems on the verge of breaking, the Nuevo León native was singing Lights of New York. Pedro Rodríguez had resisted becoming his dealer. But his credit was worthless in San Pedroslavia. The only way to surround himself with drugs was to sell them.

When the needle on the record player changed positions, it cut the drug's sweet effect off from Pedro Rodríguez's body. He immediately fell into a state of cold turkey. He opened his eyes and a pack of dogs like a roving mob showed up next to his bed. The vertigo he'd experience trying to get off the mattress made him much more anxious than the pain in his joints. The certainty that the dogs would tear him apart kept him clinging to the wall by his fingernails.

Terrified, he brought his face over to the edge of the bed. He ascertained that the dogs were running around. Rabid dogs. More than a hundred of them. With fear in his eyes, and his eyes on the very rim of the mattress, Pedro Rodríguez emitted an extraordinary shriek, and then, one by one, the one-hundred-seventeen dogs jumped into his chest with all the contractions that foreshadowed a spasm. When he swallowed the last animal, it was nighttime and the Juan Salazar LP was playing over and over.

Juan Salucita Salazar settled on Orizaba Street, #210-8, in San Pedroslavia. Huncke, who was an old hand at extraditions and had burglary charges pending, had decided to stay with Bill Garver and rejected outright the move to Mexico. Juan Salucita arrived accompanied by another Juan, John Vollmer, a beat poet. And a junky too. Metrohomosexual. The singer's lover.

It was no secret Vollmer was a fag. Ross Russell had revealed it in the unauthorized biography of the singer,

Salucita Lives: The High Life and Hard Times of Juan (an implosition) Salazar (Charterhouse, New York, 19—). It's a common quality assigned to mythic characters. His legend has a place in eternity. There shouldn't be any other readings of Juan Salazar's genius, just those that reflect his revolutionary contributions to the world of music. Reputable critics such as Charles Delaunay, Ted Gioia, Joachim Berendt, and Leonard Feather have defended his sexual preference by citing the creativity of his norteño improvisations. The fascination with Juan Salazar, aside from his being a jazzman committed to amarillo, is the allegory that produces his art. The pride of the post-norteño condition is its violent, sexist, and senseless character, almost like hip hop's. The allegory lies in the fact that, in a macho society, a fag would, under his lice-egg leather boots, wear pink polish on his toenails and still be the object of so much masculine admiration. Juan Salazar is a bebop norteño transgressor.

San Pedroslavia coincided with the epistemology of bar stories. The healthy atmosphere surrounding the daily routine of heating up spoonfuls of drugs helped Juan form a new quintet with local musicians. The problem of the pistol remained—struck by a case of nerves, Juan

Salazar couldn't say farewell to it—but he had a possible buyer: Pedro Rodríguez, a dealer famous for wearing a piteado belt with a steel buckle. He'd heard he could find him at the Laguna Coliseum, the old Sports Palace, a wrestling arena.

To get the drug, Pedro Rodríguez had to give up his Cowboy Bible. He traded it at a flea market. They tossed it into a corner with an accordion and a bajo sexto. He invested the money in heroin, which he hid in Nescafé jars between the dogs and the bed.

He began dealing by the balloonful, but that quantity was too expensive for junkies, who barely live day-to-day. The solution rested with *chinches*: single doses. But the profits were limited. San Pedroslavia is a City of Vice, and every three houses somebody offers you drugs. If you don't want to bother, you can go straight to a shooting gallery where, for twenty pesos, you stretch out your arm, they apply a tourniquet, and the dealers themselves inject you. While the others dealt via windows, Pedro Rodríguez used the old mule system. He'd deliver the drugs straight to the home. His clientele were the addicts who didn't want to move. They were few in number. Nonetheless, there were enough earnings so he'd never lack his own personal spoonful.

Pedro Rodríguez was a huge wrestling fan. Each Sunday, he'd go to the Laguna Coliseum. He was a rudo. His father had been a wrestler: The Blue Shadow. He lamented having lost The Cowboy Bible. The wrestling arena made him remember. It was there he found The Cowboy Bible, abandoned, broken, worn; a musician had stepped all over it after having traveled with it under a train seat. In the end, if they haven't been destroyed, instruments should be pawned or sold to get drugs.

WILLIAM TELL'S CORRIDO

—Thank you very much. Luis Ernesto Martínez on the saxophone. Dr. Benway on drums. Clark-Nova on the bajo sexto. Dave Tesorero on accordion.

—On the mic: Juan Salazar.

The Bunker, a blues bar, was oversold. The crowd could not accept that the band was not coming back for a second encore. Juan Juan Juan, screamed the pickpockets, always among the most passionate fans. Pedro Rodríguez had a seat at the third table. He knew the group wasn't coming back onstage when he saw a tech guy approaching him. He got up to go with him back to the dressing room, but some staff guy said, Not here. Juan's waiting for you at this address and handed him a piece of paper with directions.

The info on the napkin didn't indicate 210-8 Orizaba Street. Instead, there were directions to a bar called The Other Paradise. The place was sordid, and the clientele was subdued. It was a junky bar, with a dirt floor and wooden tables. The bar was on the left. The curtain to the bathroom was made from long strips of matchbox tops threaded together. In the back, near the jukebox, a concrete stairway led to the second floor.

Pedro Rodríguez entered the bar and took a seat at a table facing the back. There were only three customers. Two at one table were getting ready to shoot up. The other guy muttered before a bottle of sotol. Ten minutes went by and the bartender still hadn't offered him a drink.

He was about to order a Superior beer when Juan Salazar appeared at the top of the stairs. The bar lighting changed. Everything became a sandy color: the bar, the barman, Juan Salazar's tie.

He began to descend the stairs, and time turned to rubber. Pedro Rodríguez sensed something different in his walk. He thought maybe it had something to do with the exaggerated care he was taking in coming down, but no. It was confirmed when he arrived on even ground. He was walking stiffly. Each step was in the form of a square. Every two steps, he'd change directions. He seemed more like a car trying to park than a man approaching his destination. He seemed indecisive. Pixelated. Yes, a pixelated Juan Salazar was nearing his table.

He sat down across from him, but his image seemed to be experiencing some sort of interference. It was as if his signal was getting lost. His tie resembled transistors. Behind him, the linked bottle-top curtain at the front door clattered when a customer entered the bar. They got up and started up to the second floor. Pedro Rodríguez couldn't recall if the singer had said a single word.

John Vollmer was waiting for them in a little room. There was a Cowboy Bible in the corner. Pedro Rodríguez took it out of its case and began to play a polka. He paused to present his newest album. John Vollmer asked him how long he'd been playing. Since I was a boy. Juan would love to ask him to join the quintet but, unfortunately, they had a complete group; if the current guy screwed up though, they'd contract Pedro. Juan prepared the drug, and all three shot up.

When the drug's intensity began to fade, John Vollmer and Juan Salazar began to fuck. Pedro Rodríguez remained on a rocking chair by himself. Given his position, he couldn't see them, but he could hear them moaning. He looked under the rocker and saw them. He saw the dogs. They were there. It couldn't be. I'm not cold turkey. This isn't my room. He leaned down again and recognized his bed, the phrase written on the wall. The dogs were organizing a hunt.

When the lovers finished fucking, the dogs overpowered Pedro Rodríguez.

—It's time for the William Tell routine.

The apartment where Juan Salazar was unbuttoning his jacket was in the Monterrey Building. The meeting was to celebrate their recording of Mi último refugio with a string accompaniment. The boys in the band, the sound engineers, and a marquis, who, it was rumored, was after the singer's bones, were toasting with Torrecillas sotol.

—It's time for the William Tell number, Juan Salazar said again.

He was drunk, and the first thing every norteño in love wants to do once they're intoxicated is prove what a good shot they are. He left his jacket on the couch, rolled up his sleeves, loosened his tie, and undid the safety on the Star .380. John Vollmer raised a half-full glass of sotol and coyly placed it on his head. The singer stepped back about two or three meters and aimed.

He pulled the trigger and fired. Both the glass and John Vollmer fell to the floor. Turning in concentric circles on top of the blue tiles, the glass revealed itself intact. A puddle of blood emerged on John Vollmer's forehead. With tears on his face, Juan Salazar bent down to his lover. Juanito, Juanito, talk to me, talk to me, don't die, Juanito, don't die. The game had gone wrong. John Vollmer was dead. The bullet wound sparkled on his forehead.

*

Pedro Rodríguez woke up with half his body spilling out from under the blankets. There were no dogs in the room. The sun indicated it was noon. It was Botanus time. Plenty to be thankful for. The desert's caress could be felt at about forty-two degrees Celsius in the shade.

It may have been inappropriate, but he wanted to eat. With blurred vision, hair on end and shaky hands, he managed to make it to the fridge. The first thing he swallowed was a jar of mayo. Without checking the expiration date, without a clue as to how long it had been there, he spooned it with his finger without a thought. Then he opened a can of Brunswick sardines, which he could tell by the smell had aged well beyond four weeks. Then he went on to a jar of Valentina sauce. Down to the bottom. For dessert, he had a first-aid gel he found in the freezer.

Still hungry, he directed himself to the bathroom, with the idea of drinking Vaseline, but the chill kept him from it. Trembling, he closed his eyes and crouched by the wall. A blanket, he cried. Someone give me a blanket! His screams were useless. Damn dogs. There was no one in the room who could offer him shelter. Just him and those forty-two degrees. A blanket! I'm dying from the cold. And so, trembling and naked, he fell asleep. With no one to help him, he couldn't even cover himself: He was too far from the bed.

With the shoebox under his arm, Juan Salazar entered the building. He rang the attic-room doorbell. Pedro Rodríguez opened the door. His skin had red splotches all over it. Scotland.

—Pedro.

—Yes, Juan.

—I need two grams of heroin. But I don't have the money to pay you.

—Juan, you know... it's business.

—I brought this. He showed him the Star .380.

—That changes things. Given that, we don't have to take the usual steps.

—Juan handed Pedro the gun, wrapped in a handkerchief and still warm from the shot that had killed John Vollmer, then took the drug and made his way down the dirty boulevard. Pedro Rodríguez stayed in his room, scratching. The itching was so intense that all through the wee hours the only sound on the streets was that of his nails on his skin.

THE COWBOY BIBLE

At the station, the commissioner reprimanded two of his agents.

—What's this about you refusing to arrest Pedro Rodríguez?

—We've heard stories, commissioner.

—Damn.

—They say he's a *nahual.*

—What's that?

—A witch. An Indian witch who can transform himself into a bird, bubble, fire, coyote, or whatever he wants.

—Those are stories told by ignorant people. Do you think this is a movie? Pedro Rodríguez is nothing more than an insignificant dealer.

—They say they've seen him shoot with a Cowboy Bible.

—Don't be ridiculous. A Cowboy Bible? So, what then, he uses a guitar to cut onions?

—Commissioner...

—Don't commissioner me. You two get out of here and get that asshole by whatever means necessary.

*

—Don't make me lose my patience. Just confess, Mr. Juan Salazar. What did you do with the gun that killed your lover? asked the commissioner.

—I already told you. I gave it to Pedro Rodríguez.

—For the last time, Mr. Juan Salazar: Do you know where to find Pedro Rodríguez?

Juan Salazar was detained at Lecumberri for only thirteen days. He was released on bail. Court costs were $2,312. His attorney, Bernabé Jurado, charged $2,300 for his services, $300 of which were used to bribe the boys in ballistics. When they couldn't find the murder weapon, Jurado substituted a Smith & Wesson for the Star .380 so as not to delay the proceedings. The whole story about the William Tell game was proven false. The version presented in court asserted that Juan Salazar was cleaning his weapon. The gun accidentally fell to the floor and fired. The bullet entered the victim's forehead without premeditation.

John Vollmer was buried in grave #1018-A in the Panteón Americano.

*

Pedro Rodríguez was listening to the blues on his old record player when they rang the doorbell of his attic room. He thought about the cops, he thought about the dogs, and he thought about Juan Salazar. With the needle still hanging off his arm, he got up to see who it was. It was nobody. And before some Yankee showed up with his imported boner, insisting on trading it for drugs, he grabbed the Star .380 and went out on the streets.

He arrived at the Laguna Coliseum in time for the second fight. That night, there was a mask vs. hairpiece match between Santo's Son and Menace Jr. He bought some snacks and a Victoria beer. When it came time for the superdeluxe semifinal, after he'd had four beers, he saw a narc guarding the men's bathroom. A second stood at the door, and a third roamed the general ring area.

With the gun tucked into his pants waist, he made his way to the rudos dressing room. A fourth narc intercepted him. All four patted him down, but they didn't find the gun. In its place, badly hidden in his pants, they found a Cowboy Bible. After searching his attic room and driving him around in an old Dodge for two hours with his head between his legs, Pedro Rodríguez still didn't reveal the whereabouts of the Star .380. He also couldn't explain how he'd come upon The Cowboy Bible. They took him cuffed to the station. The gun was never found.

The beating ended at five in the afternoon. Two police thugs had been cracking him from eleven in the morning on, hoping he'd let loose the 411 on the gun's whereabouts. Disconcerted by his stubborn silence, they dropped him back in his cell so that after a brief rest and a chat, he'd recover his ability to feel pain, so that he wouldn't forget what it felt like, so that he wouldn't miss it.

At seven they brought him dinner. It was already dark because of the summer change in time zones. He could hear music coming from the central plaza. He'd be transferred to Lecumberri the next day. The torture sessions left him exhausted, and he fell asleep with his eyes fixed on the wall.

Some goings-on in the cell woke him up. When he was sleeping, he dreamed of saxophones: tenors, altos, sopranos. He imagined the band's revelry, he even thought he heard When the Saints Go Marching In. But the noise in the cell wouldn't let him concentrate on the melody. He imagined the cops would be coming back for another round. What are they waiting for, he asked himself. But it wasn't them. He remembered the dogs. He was sure it was the dogs, but he refused to look.

He kept his face to the wall. He heard a voice in his head, and he was afraid. There they are again, the voice said. Because of the din, he assumed the dogs were playing around. The voice spoke again: There they are again, and those bastards don't understand. Pedro Rodríguez turned to look. They weren't dogs but men, and they had gathered in a circle like a group of boys kicking around a ball on fire. He got up from the cot and moved to the center of the circle.

How can I be afraid of them, if they're a part of me, he said, as if he was talking back to the voice inside him. Then the one hundred and seventeen men all began to jump inside him with a long wail.

The guards on duty woke from the riot.

—Go get him, the new guy's acting out. Quick, before he hangs himself.

But when the guards on duty looked through the bars, they didn't see the prisoner. The lock was still locked.

The only thing in the cell was a snake that glittered like a cowboy belt.

—Look, partner. A snake.

—Kill it, kill it. Shoot it, you dummy. It's a Masticophis flagellum. They nest in houses.

They pulled out their guns and opened fire on the snake that slithered and crawled, slithered and crawled, slithered and crawled. When they were sure it was dead, the opened the cell door, but there was absolutely no trace of the creature. In its place they found only a piteado belt shot through with bullet holes.

EPILOGUE I

EMILIO SAYS to The Cowboy Bible, You can consider this goodbye. With what's due you, you can restart your life. I'm going to San Francisco, with the one who's everything to me.

Four shots were heard. The Cowboy Bible had killed Emilio. The police found only a discarded gun. No one heard anything ever again about the money or The Cowboy Bible.

EPILOGUE II

LATER, AT DAWN, SHE TOLD ME:

—You're a loser, Old Paulino. You're not at all affectionate. You know who was sweet to me?

—Who?

—The Cowboy Bible. He really knew how to make love.

ABOUT THE AUTHOR

Born in Coahuila, Mexico, in 1978, CARLOS VELÁZQUEZ is the author of story collections *Cuco Sánchez Blues* (2004), *La Biblia Vaquera* (named one of the books of the year by *Reforma* in 2009), and *La marrana negra de la literatura rosa* (2010). He received the Premio Nacional de Cuento Magdalena Mondragón and has been anthologized in El Fondo de Cultura Económica's *Anuario de poesia mexicana 2007*.

ABOUT THE TRANSLATOR

Born in Havana, Cuba, ACHY OBEJAS has written fiction, poetry, and journalism. She is the author of five books, including three novels: *Days of Awe*, *Memory Mambo*, and *Ruins*. Her poetry chapbook, *This Is What Happened in Our Other Life*, was both a critical favorite and a bestseller. She is trained as a journalist and has worked in the alternative press, including *In These Times*, where she writes a monthly column, and the *Chicago Tribune*. A translator between Spanish and English, she translated into Spanish Junot Díaz's *The Brief Wondrous Life of Oscar Wao* and *This Is How You Lose Her* and into English such contemporary Latin American writers as Rita Indiana, F. G. Haghenbeck, and Wendy Guerra. She is the recipient of a USA Ford Fellowship, a Woodrow Wilson Visiting Fellowship, a team Pulitzer Prize for the series "Gateway to Gridlock" while at the *Tribune*, a National Endowment for the Arts Fellowship in poetry, the Studs Terkel Journalism Award, and a Cintas Foundation Fellowship. She is currently the Distinguished Visiting Writer at Mills College in Oakland, California.

RESTLESS BOOKS is an independent publisher for readers and writers in search of new destinations, experiences, and perspectives. From Asia to the Americas, from Tehran to Tel Aviv, we deliver stories of discovery, adventure, dislocation, and transformation.

Our readers are passionate about other cultures and other languages. Restless is committed to bringing out the best of international literature—fiction, journalism, memoirs, poetry, travel writing, illustrated books, and more—that reflects the restlessness of our multiform lives.